SLEEPING BEAUTY

AND OTHER TALES OF SLUMBERING PRINCESSES

Amelia Carruthers

Origins of Fairy Tales
from Around the World

POOK  PRESS

Copyright © 2015 Pook Press
An imprint of Read Publishing Ltd.
Home Farm, 44 Evesham Road, Cookhill, Alcester,
Warwickshire, B49 5LJ

Introduced and edited by Amelia Carruthers.
Cover design by Zoë Horn Haywood.
Design by Zoë Horn Haywood and Sam Bigland.

British Library Cataloguing-in-Publication Data. A
catalogue record for this book is available from the
British Library.

Contents

An Introduction to the Fairy Tale 1

The History of *Sleeping Beauty* 5

THE DOOMED PRINCE

(An Egyptian Tale) 9

SIGURD AND BRYNHILD

(An Icelandic Tale) 19

SOLE, LUNA, E TALIA

(An Italian Tale) 27

LA BELLE AU BOIS DORMANT

(A French Tale) 39

DORNRÖNSCHEN

(A German Tale) 63

LITTLE SURYA BAI

(An Indian Tale) 73

THE KING OF ENGLAND AND HIS THREE SONS

(An English Tale) 103

The Golden Age of Illustration 131

An Introduction to
the Fairy Tale

Fairy Tales are told in almost every society, all over the globe. They have the ability to inspire generations of young and old alike, yet fail to fit neatly into any one mode of storytelling. Today, most people know these narratives through literary works or even film versions, but this is a far cry from the genre's early development. Most of the stories began, and are still propagated through oral traditions, which are still very much alive in certain cultures. Especially in rural, poorer regions, the telling of tales – from village to village, or from elder to younger, preserves culture and custom, whilst still enabling the teller to vary, embellish or adapt the tale as they see fit.

To provide a brief attempt at definition, a fairy tale is a type of short story that typically features 'fantasy' characters, such as dwarves, elves, fairies, giants, gnomes, goblins, mermaids, trolls or witches, and usually magic or enchantments to boot! Fairy tales may be distinguished from other folk narratives such as legends (which generally involve belief in the veracity of the events described) and explicitly moral tales, including fables or those of a religious nature. In cultures where demons and witches are perceived as real, fairy tales may merge into legends, where the narrative is perceived both by teller and hearers as being grounded in historical truth. However unlike legends and epics, they usually do not contain more than superficial references to religion and actual places, people, and events; they take place 'once upon a time' rather than in reality.

The history of the fairy tale is particularly difficult to trace, as most often, it is only the literary forms that are available to the scholar. Still, written evidence indicates that fairy tales have existed for thousands of years, although not perhaps recognized as a genre. Many of today's fairy narratives have evolved from centuries-old stories that have appeared, with variations, in multiple cultures around the world. Two theories of origins have attempted to explain the common elements in fairy tales across continents. One is that a single point of origin generated any given tale, which then spread over the centuries. The other is that such fairy tales stem from common human experience and therefore can appear separately in many different origins. Debates still rage over which interpretation is correct, but as ever, it is likely that a combination of both aspects are involved in the advancements of these folkloric chronicles.

Some folklorists prefer to use the German term *Märchen* or 'wonder tale' to refer to the genre over *fairy tale,* a practice given weight by the definition of Thompson in his 1977 edition of *The Folktale.* He described it as 'a tale of some length involving a succession of motifs or episodes. It moves in an unreal world without definite locality or definite creatures and is filled with the marvellous. In this never-never land, humble heroes kill adversaries, succeed to kingdoms and marry princesses.' The genre was first marked out by writers of the Renaissance, such as Giovanni Francesco Straparola and Giambattista Basile, and stabilized through the works of later collectors such as Charles Perrault and the Brothers Grimm. The oral tradition of the fairy tale came long before the written page however.

Tales were told or enacted dramatically, rather than written down, and handed from generation to generation. Because of this, many fairy tales appear in written literature throughout different cultures, as in *The Golden Ass,* which includes *Cupid and Psyche* (Roman, 100–200 CE), or the *Panchatantra* (India, 3rd century CE). However it is still unknown to what extent these reflect the actual folk tales even of their own time. The 'fairy tale' as a genre became popular among the French nobility of the seventeenth century, and among the tales told were the *Contes* of Charles Perrault (1697), who fixed the forms of 'Sleeping Beauty' and 'Cinderella.' Perrault largely laid the foundations for this new literary variety, with some of the best of his works including 'Puss in Boots', 'Little Red Riding Hood' and 'Bluebeard'.

The first collectors to attempt to preserve not only the plot and characters of the tale, but also the style in which they were told were the Brothers Grimm, who assembled German fairy tales. The Brothers Grimm rejected several tales for their anthology, though told by Germans, because the tales derived from Perrault and they concluded that the stories were thereby *French* and not *German* tales. An oral version of 'Bluebeard' was thus rejected, and the tale of 'Little Briar Rose', clearly related to Perrault's 'The Sleeping Beauty' was included only because Jacob Grimm convinced his brother that the figure of *Brynhildr*, from much earlier Norse mythology, proved that the sleeping princess was authentically German. The Grimm Brothers remain some of the best-known story-tellers of folk tales though, popularising 'Hansel and Gretel', 'Rapunzel', 'Rumplestiltskin' and 'Snow White.'

The work of the Brothers Grimm influenced other collectors, both inspiring them to collect tales and leading them to similarly believe, in a spirit of romantic nationalism, that the fairy tales of a country were particularly representative of it (unfortunately generally ignoring any cross-cultural references). Among those influenced were the Norwegian Peter Christen Asbjørnsen (*Norske Folkeeventyr*, 1842-3), the Russian Alexander Afanasyev (*Narodnye Russkie Skazki,* 1855-63) and the Englishman, Joseph Jacobs (*English Fairy Tales*, 1890). Simultaneously to such developments, writers such as Hans Christian Andersen and George MacDonald continued the tradition of penning original literary fairy tales. Andersen's work sometimes drew on old folktales, but more often deployed fairytale motifs and plots in new stories; for instance in 'The Little Mermaid', 'The Ugly Duckling' and 'The Emperor's New Clothes.'

Fairy tales are still written in the present day, attesting to their enormous popularity and cultural longevity. Aside from their long and diverse literary history, these stories have also been stunningly illustrated by some of the world's best artists – as the reader will be able to see in the following pages. The Golden Age of Illustration (a period customarily defined as lasting from the latter quarter of the nineteenth century until just after the First World War) produced some of the finest examples of this craft, and the masters of the trade are all collected in this volume, alongside the original, inspiring tales. These images form their own story, evolving in conjunction with the literary development of the tales. Consequently, the illustrations are presented in their own narrative sequence, for the reader to appreciate *in and of themselves*. An introduction to the 'Golden Age' can also be found at the end of this book.

The History of Sleeping Beauty

The tale of *Sleeping Beauty* is one of the classics of the fairy-tale genre, with a truly fascinating history. Alongside stories such as *Cinderella* and *Little Red Riding Hood*, it is one of the best known narratives in the western-European tradition, but arguably originates from much further afield. The story essentially revolves around a beautiful princess, an enchantment of sleep and a handsome prince. So far so simple. But as a result of her many adaptations, appropriations and re-tellings, the *Sleeping Beauty* has, over time, undertaken a considerable transformation.

The idea of a child, cursed at birth and subsequently shut in isolation for their own protection is incredibly old, but there are few tales which utilize this trope directly. The first widely known example is connected with the Ancient Egyptian belief in the Fates (or Hathors), who attended the bedside of an Egyptian Queen and predicted the fortunes of her newly born child. In the tale of *The Doomed Prince,* the child is a boy, and his fate is not threatened by spindles or flax, but 'his death is to be by the crocodile, or by the serpent or by the dog.' Similarly to later *Sleeping Beauty* narratives though, the king builds a great royal house in the desert, in order to protect his newly born child. The ending of this tale, copied from the *Great Harris Papyrus* (at forty-one metres, the longest known papyrus from ancient Egypt, with some 1,500 lines of text) is unfortunately unknown. It thus forms one of the great folkloric mysteries, of how exactly *The Doomed Prince* may, or may not, escape his fate.

Other early influences could have come from the story of the sleeping Brynhild in the *Saga of the Völsungs* (a thirteenth century Icelandic prose narrative). Here, Sigurd is instructed to 'ride to Hundarfell, where the fair Brynhild lies asleep.' Brynhild was the daughter of a famous king, herself famous for her beauty and wisdom, but was punished with eternal slumber after an angered Odin (the ruler of Asgard) struck her with a sleeping thorn. This is perhaps more similar to the 'Sleeping Beauty' storyline as we know it than the Egyptian legend; although both are equally intriguing. The first version to have a truly substantial narrative similarity is a fourteenth century tale though, the rendition of *L'histoire de Troylus et de la belle Zellandine,* penned in French by an anonymous author. This appeared in the prose romance *Perceforest,* which, although written in French, was composed in the Low Countries between 1330 and 1344. An Episode contained in 'Book III, Chapter iii', depicts the prince Troylus coming across the sleeping Zellandine, raping her, and Zelladine subsequently giving birth without waking.

This medieval narrative, a shocking forebear for many modern readers, has striking parallels with the first full-length Sleeping Beauty tale, that of the Italian Giambattista Basile; *Sole, Luna, e Talia,* published in 1634. Basile's telling is also the most likely influence on Charles Perrault's *La Belle au Bois Dormant* (1697) which fixed the narrative as we know it today. In the early Italian version, the first part of the story corresponds with the earlier narratives of *Troylus et de la belle Zellandine* and Sigurd and Brynhild – but the second half takes the story into new territory. The first part tells of the birth of Princess Talia, and the soothsayers warning of 'a great peril awaiting her from a piece of stalk in some flax' (similar to Odin's sleeping thorn, and the Hathor's prophecy). Despite the King's best efforts to keep her isolated and safe, Talia meets this misfortune, and falls into an enchanted sleep. After being found and 'admired' by a travelling King, Talia is later stumbled upon by two young children (analogously representing the childbirth of Zellandine), one of whom wakes the princess by sucking out the flax. The second part then goes on to recount how the King's step-mother, becoming jealous, attempts to cook and serve the two children (named sun and moon) to the King, and throw Talia on the fire. The plan is foiled though, and the step-mother is suitably punished.

Perrault's tale follows the same narrative pattern, and he even goes so far as to call the two children L'Aurore (Dawn) and Le Jour (Day) in a nod to Basile's story. In the second half of this variant, the step-mother is actually an ogre, and the Prince and the Princess had got married in secret. Some scholars believe that these two halves were originally entirely separate tales, and consequently, the Brothers Grimm – ever the consummate folklorists, decided to represent this separation in their collection. Their tale of *Little Briar Rose* (1812), who falls into the enchanted sleep after a prick from a spindle, ends (like the original tellings) when the prince arrives to wake the sleeping beauty. Unusually for the Brothers Grimm, their story is one of the tamest of the 'sleeping beauty' narratives, with none of the attempted cannibalism, adultery or rape found in earlier renditions. The Brothers considered rejecting the story on the grounds that it was derived from Perrault's version, but the presence of Brynhild in the Norse sagas convinced them to include it as an *authentically German* tale.

The incident of the sleep-thorn (the prick from the spindle) is also found in a Southern Indian tale, that of *Little Surya Bai*. This formed part of Mary Frere's *Old Deccan Days* (1868), a collection of stories taken from oral traditions in Southern India. In this version, it is a splinter coming out of the wall of an Eagle's cage, that causes the young girl to fall down senseless – before being rescued and married by a Rajah. Here, the story's 'second half is included, and the 'sleeping beauty' becomes the victim of jealously not by her mother-in-law, but of another wife. Like Basile and Perrault's narratives, the wicked first wife is eventually punished, and Surya Bai and the Rajah live happily for the rest of their days.

As a testament to this tale's ability to inspire and entertain generations of readers, the story of *The Sleeping Beauty* continues to influence popular culture internationally. With a massive geographical range, it lends plot elements, allusions and tropes to a wide variety of artistic mediums. It has been translated into almost every language, and very excitingly, is continuing to evolve in the present day. We hope the reader enjoys this collection of some of its best re-tellings.

As much surprised as she to learn the fish she rescued was a fairy!

An Old Fairy Tale - The Sleeping Beauty, 1868.

Illustrated by The Dalziel Brothers

THE DOOMED PRINCE

(An Egyptian Tale)

The Doomed Prince comes from a collection published in 1895, titled *Egyptian Tales, translated from the papyri; Second Series, XVIIIth to XIXth Dynasty,* authored by Sir William Mathews Flinders Petrie (1853 - 1942). Petrie held the first chair of Egyptology in the United Kingdom, and excavated many of the most important archaeological sites in Egypt in conjunction with his wife, Hilda Petrie. The stories encompassed in his volume came from the *Great Harris Papyrus,* found in a tomb near Medinet Habu, across the Nile river from Luxor, Egypt. It is thought to have been written soon after the reign of Ramses III, who lived from 1217 - 1155 BCE.

This tale, although immediately different from later, better known variants of the 'Sleeping Beauty' narrative (chiefly at variance in the sex of the protagonist), does contain many striking similarities. Firstly, the royal couple receive a grave prophecy from 'the hathors' (akin to the three fates, or later, fairies and soothsayers). On hearing this, the King attempts to keep his infant son safe, by isolating him in a great castle in the desert. How the young Prince escapes (or indeed, succumbs to) his fate is unknown however, as Petrie's papyrus abruptly ends before the story has reached its conclusion.

There once was a king to whom no son was born; and his heart was grieved, and he prayed for himself unto the gods around him for a child. They decreed that one should be born to him. And his wife, after her time was fulfilled, brought forth a son. Then came the Hathors to decree for him a destiny; they said, "His death is to be by the crocodile, or by the serpent, or by the dog." Then the people who stood by heard this, and they went to tell it to his majesty. Then his majesty's heart sickened very greatly. And his majesty caused a house to be built upon the desert; it was furnished with people and with all good things of the royal house, that the child should not go abroad. And when the child was grown, he went up upon the roof, and he saw a dog; it was following a man who was walking on the road. He spoke to his page, who was with him, "What is this that walks behind the man who is coming along the road?" He answered him, "This is a dog." The child said to him, "Let there be brought to me one like it." The page went to repeat it to his majesty. And his majesty said, "Let there be brought to him a little pet dog, lest his heart be sad." And behold they brought to him the dog.

Then when the days increased after this, and when the child became grown in all his limbs, he sent a message to his father saying, "Come, wherefore am I kept here? Inasmuch as I am fated to three evil fates, let me follow my desire. Let God do what is in His heart." They agreed to all he said, and gave him all sorts of arms, and also his dog to follow him, and they took him to the east country, and said to him, "Behold, go thou whither thou wilt." His dog was with him, and he went northward, following his heart in the desert, while he lived on all the best of the game of the desert. He went to the chief of Naharaina.

And behold there had not been any born to the chief of Naharaina, except one daughter. Behold, there had been built for her a house; its seventy windows were seventy cubits from the ground. And the chief caused to be brought all the sons of the chiefs of the land of Khalu, and said to them, "He who reaches the window of my daughter, she shall be to him for a wife."

It is to have a small child of your own.
The Sleeping Beauty, 1920.
Illustrated by Arthur Rackham

The King could not contain himself for joy.
Snowdrop and Other Tales, 1920.
Illustrated by Arthur Rackham

And many days after these things, as they were in their daily task, the youth rode by the place where they were. They took the youth to their house, they bathed him, they gave provender to his horses, they brought all kinds of things for the youth, they perfumed him, they anointed his feet, they gave him portions of their own food; and they spake to him, "Whence comest thou, goodly youth?" He said to them, "I am son of an officer of the land of Egypt; my mother is dead, and my father has taken another wife. And when she bore children, she grew to hate me, and I have come as a fugitive from before her." And they embraced him, and kissed him.

And after many days were passed, he said to the youths, "What is it that ye do here?" And they said to him, "We spend our time in this: we climb up, and he who shall reach the window of the daughter of the chief of Naharaina, to him will he given her to wife." He said to them, "If it please you, let me behold the matter, that I may come to climb with you." They went to climb, as was their daily wont: and the youth stood afar off to behold; and the face of the daughter of the chief of Naharaina was turned to them. And another day the sons came to climb, and the youth came to climb with the sons of the chiefs. He climbed, and he reached the window of the daughter of the chief of Naharaina. She kissed him, she embraced him in all his limbs.

And one went to rejoice the heart of her father, and said to him, "One of the people has reached the window of thy daughter." And the prince inquired of the messenger, saying, "The son of which of the princes is it?" And he replied to him, "It is the son of an officer, who has come as a fugitive from the land of Egypt, fleeing from before his stepmother when she had children." Then the chief of Naharaina was exceeding angry; and he said, "Shall I indeed give my daughter to the Egyptian fugitive? Let him go back whence he came." And one came to tell the youth, "Go back to the place thou earnest from." But the maiden seized his hand; she swore an oath by God, saying, "By the being of Ra Harakhti, if one takes him from me, I will not eat, I will not drink, I shall die in that same hour." The messenger went to tell unto her father all that she said. Then the prince sent men to slay the youth, while he was in his house. But the maiden said, "By the being of Ra, if one slay him I shall be dead ere the sun goeth down. I will not pass an hour of life if I am parted from him." And one went to tell her father. Then the prince made them bring the youth with the maiden. The youth was seized with fear when he came before the prince. But he embraced him, he kissed him all over, and said, "Oh! tell me who thou art; behold, thou art to me as a son." He said to him, "I am a son of an officer of the land of Egypt; my mother died, my father took to him a second wife; she came to hate me, and I fled a fugitive from before her." He then gave to him his daughter to wife; he gave also to him a house, and serfs, and fields, also cattle and all manner of good things.

But after the days of these things were passed, the youth said to his wife, "I am doomed to three fates—a crocodile, a serpent, and a dog." She said to him, "Let one kill the dog which belongs to thee." He replied to her, "I am not going to kill my dog, which I have brought up from when it was small." And she feared greatly for her husband, and would not let him go alone abroad.

And one went with the youth toward the land of Egypt, to travel in that country. Behold the crocodile of the river, he came out by the town in which the youth was. And in that town was a mighty man. And the mighty man would not suffer the crocodile to escape. And when the crocodile was bound, the mighty man went out and walked abroad. And when the sun rose the mighty man went back to the house; and he did so every day, during two months of days.

Now when the days passed after this, the youth sat making a good day in his house.

At the christening the princess had seven fairies for her godmothers.

The Sleeping Beauty, 1895.

Illustrated by R. Anning Bell

All the fairies in the land came to the christening.
Fairy Tales, 1915.
Illustrated by Margaret Tarrant

And when the evening came he lay down on his bed, sleep seized upon his limbs; and his wife filled a bowl of milk, and placed it by his side. Then came out a serpent from his hole, to bite the youth; behold his wife was sitting by him, she lay not down. Thereupon the servants gave milk to the serpent, and he drank, and was drunk, and lay upside down. Then his wife made it to perish with the blows of her dagger. And they woke her husband, who was astonished; and she said unto him, "Behold thy God has given one of thy dooms into thy hand; He will also give thee the others." And he sacrificed to God, adoring Him, and praising His spirits from day to day.

And when the days were passed after these things, the youth went to walk in the fields of his domain. He went not alone, behold his dog was following him. And his dog ran aside after the wild game, and he followed the dog. He came to the river, and entered the river behind his dog. Then came out the crocodile, and took him to the place where the mighty man was. And the crocodile said to the youth, "I am thy doom, following after thee. ..."

[Here the papyrus breaks off.]

The old fairy's spite.
The Sleeping Beauty, 1912.
Illustrated by John Hassall

SIGURD AND BRYNHILD

(An Icelandic Tale)

The following tale is a short extract from the *Saga of the Völsungs*, a legendary thirteenth century Icelandic prose rendition of the origin and decline of the Völsung clan. It is made up of forty chapters in total, but the story of Sigurd and Brynhild first appears in 'Chapter Twenty' (below). The earliest known pictorial representation of this tradition is the Ramsund carving, in Sweden, which was created around 1000 CE. The origins of most of the material are thought to be much older however, as the story echoes real events in Central Europe during the Migration period, chiefly the destruction of the Burgundian kingdom in the fifth century.

In the following chapter, titled *Sigurd's Meeting with Brynhild on the Mountain*, Sigurd 'the Dragon Slayer' discovers and wakes the fair Brynhild who was suffering an eternal sleep. Foreshadowing later descriptions of the prick from a spindle, splinter or piece of flax, Brynhild was struck by Odin's 'sleep thorn', after she incited his wrath. The character of Brynhild is far removed from modern depictions of the helpless, sleeping princess though – she is a 'shieldmaiden' (a warrior woman), who pledges herself in marriage to Sigurd, but also prophesises his eventual doom.

By long roads rides Sigurd, till he comes at the last up on to Hindfell, and wends his way south to the land of the Franks; and he sees before him on the fell a great light, as of fire burning, and flaming up even unto the heavens; and when he came thereto, lo, a shield-hung castle before him, and a banner on the topmost thereof: into the castle went Sigurd, and saw one lying there asleep, and all-armed. Therewith he takes the helm from off the head of him, and sees that it is no man, but a woman; and she was clad in a byrny as closely set on her as though it had grown to her flesh; so he rent it from the collar downwards; and then the sleeves thereof, and ever the sword bit on it as if it were cloth. Then said Sigurd that over-long had she lain asleep; but she asked—

"What thing of great might is it that has prevailed to rend my byrny, and draw me from my sleep?"

Even as sings the song:

"What bit on the byrny,
Why breaks my sleep away,
Who has turned from me
My wan tormenting?"

"Ah, is it so, that here is come Sigurd Sigmundson, bearing Fafnir's helm on his head and Fafnir's bane in his hand?"

Then answered Sigurd—

"Sigmund's son
With Sigurd's sword
E'en now rent down
The raven's wall."

On the day when she reaches her fifteenth birthday, the princess shall prick her finger with the spindle of a spinning-wheel, and shall immediately die!

The Sleeping Beauty, 1920.

Illustrated by Arthur Rackham

"Of the Volsung's kin is he who has done the deed; but now I have heard that thou art daughter of a mighty king, and folk have told us that thou wert lovely and full of lore, and now I will try the same."

Then Brynhild sang—

> "Long have I slept
>   And slumbered long,
>   Many and long are the woes of mankind,
>   By the might of Odin
>   Must I bide helpless
>   To shake from off me the spells of slumber.
>
> "Hail to the day come back!
>   Hail, sons of the daylight!
>   Hail to thee, dark night, and thy daughter!
>   Look with kind eyes a-down,
>   On us sitting here lonely,
>   And give unto us the gain that we long for.
>
> "Hail to the Aesir,
>   And the sweet Asyniur!
>   Hail to the fair earth fulfilled of plenty!
>   Fair words, wise hearts,
>   Would we win from you,
>   And healing hands while life we hold."

A spindle she through her hand shall run, and die before she be twenty-one!
An Old Fairy Tale - The Sleeping Beauty, 1868.
Illustrated by The Dalziel Brothers

The King's daughter shall in her fifteenth year be wounded by a spindle and fall down dead.

My Book of Favourite Fairy Tales, 1921.

Illustrated by Jennie Harbour

Then Brynhild speaks again and says, "Two kings fought, one hight Helm Gunnar, an old man, and the greatest of warriors, and Odin had promised the victory unto him; but his foe was Agnar, or Audi's brother: and so I smote down Helm Gunnar in the fight; and Odin, in vengeance for that deed, stuck the sleep-thorn into me, and said that I should never again have the victory, but should be given away in marriage; but thereagainst I vowed a vow, that never would I wed one who knew the name of fear."

Then said Sigurd, "Teach us the lore of mighty matters!"

At this very instant the young fairy came out from behind the hangings.
The Fairy Tales of Charles Perrault, 1922.
Illustrated by Harry Clarke

SOLE, LUNA, E TALIA

(An Italian Tale)

Sole, Luna, e Talia (Sun, Moon, and Talia) was written by Giambattista Basile (1566-1632), a Neapolitan poet and courtier. It was first published in his collection of Neapolitan fairy tales titled *Lo Cunto de li Cunti Overo lo Ttrattenemiento de Peccerille* (translating as 'The Tale of Tales, or Entertainment for Little Ones'), posthumously published in two volumes in 1634 and 1636.

Although neglected for some time, the work received a great deal of attention after the Brothers Grimm praised it highly as the first *national* collection of fairy tales. Many of the fairy tales that Basile collected are the oldest known variants in existence, including this – the first full-length printed version of the *Sleeping Beauty* narrative. The names that princess Talia chooses for her children, (Sole and Luna / Sun and Moon) actually hark back to the ancient Norse Poetic Edda (which inspired parts of the *Saga of the Völsungs*). In the first and best known poem of the Edda (*Völuspá*), the early days of the universe are recounted, in which 'the sun from the south' is the moon's eternal companion.

It is a well-known fact that the cruel man is generally his own hangman; and he who throws stones at Heaven frequently comes off with a broken head. But the reverse of the medal shows us that innocence is a shield of fig-tree wood, upon which the sword of malice is broken, or blunts its point; so that, when a poor man fancies himself already dead and buried, he revives again in bone and flesh, as you shall hear in the story which I am going to draw from the cask of memory with the tap of my tongue.

There was once a great Lord, who, having a daughter born to him named Talia, commanded the seers and wise men of his kingdom to come and tell him her fortune; and after various counsellings they came to the conclusion, that a great peril awaited her from a piece of stalk in some flax. Thereupon he issued a command, prohibiting any flax or hemp, or such-like thing, to be brought into his house, hoping thus to avoid the danger.

When Talia was grown up, and was standing one day at the window, she saw an old woman pass by who was spinning. She had never seen a distaff or a spindle, and being vastly pleased with the twisting and twirling of the thread, her curiosity was so great that she made the old woman come upstairs. Then, taking the distaff in her hand, Talia began to draw out the thread, when, by mischance, a piece of stalk in the flax getting under her finger-nail, she fell dead upon the ground; at which sight the old woman hobbled downstairs as quickly as she could.

When the unhappy father heard of the disaster that had befallen Talia, after weeping bitterly, he placed her in that palace in the country, upon a velvet seat under a canopy of brocade; and fastening the doors, he quitted for ever the place which had been the cause of such misfortune to him, in order to drive all remembrance of it from his mind.

Now, a certain King happened to go one day to the chase, and a falcon escaping from him flew in at the window of that palace. When the King found that the bird did not return at his call, he ordered his attendants to knock at the door, thinking that the palace was inhabited; and after knocking for some time, the King ordered them to fetch a vine-dresser's ladder, wishing himself to scale the house and see what was inside. Then he mounted the ladder, and

The King . . .at once published an edict.

Old Time Stories, 1921.

Illustrated by W. Heath Robinson

going through the whole palace, he stood aghast at not finding there any living person. At last he came to the room where Talia was lying, as if enchanted; and when the King saw her, he called to her, thinking that she was asleep, but in vain, for she still slept on, however loud he called. So, after admiring her beauty awhile, the King returned home to his kingdom, where for a long time he forgot all that had happened.

Meanwhile, two little twins, one a boy and the other a girl, who looked like two little jewels, wandered, from I know not where, into the palace and found Talia in a trance. At first they were afraid because they tried in vain to awaken her; but, becoming bolder, the girl gently took Talia's finger into her mouth, to bite it and wake her up by this means; and so it happened that the splinter of flax came out. Thereupon she seemed to awake as from a deep sleep; and when she saw those little jewels at her side, she took them to her heart, and loved them more than her life; but she wondered greatly at seeing herself quite alone in the palace with two children, and food and refreshment brought her by unseen hands.

After a time the King, calling Talia to mind, took occasion one day when he went to the chase to go and see her; and when he found her awakened, and with two beautiful little creatures by her side, he was struck dumb with rapture. Then the King told Talia who he was, and they formed a great league and friendship, and he remained there for several days, promising, as he took leave, to return and fetch her.

When the King went back to his own kingdom he was for ever repeating the names of Talia and the little ones, insomuch that, when he was eating he had Talia in his mouth, and Sun and Moon (for so he named the children); nay, even when he went to rest he did not leave off calling on them, first one and then the other.

And there it goes up in flames and smoke.
The Sleeping Beauty, 1920.
Illustrated by Arthur Rackham

Now the King's stepmother had grown suspicious at his long absence at the chase, and when she heard him calling thus on Talia, Sun, and Moon, she waxed wroth, and said to the King's secretary, "Hark ye, friend, you stand in great danger, between the axe and the block; tell me who it is that my stepson is enamoured of, and I will make you rich; but if you conceal the truth from me, I'll make you rue it."

The man, moved on the one side by fear, and on the other pricked by interest, which is a bandage to the eyes of honour, the blind of justice, and an old horse-shoe to trip up good faith, told the Queen the whole truth. Whereupon she sent the secretary in the King's name to Talia, saying that he wished to see the children. Then Talia sent them with great joy, but the Queen commanded the cook to kill them, and serve them up in various ways for her wretched stepson to eat.

Now the cook, who had a tender heart, seeing the two pretty little golden pippins, took compassion on them, and gave them to his wife, bidding her keep them concealed; then he killed and dressed two little kids in a hundred different ways. When the King came, the Queen quickly ordered the dishes served up; and the King fell to eating with great delight, exclaiming, "How good this is! Oh, how excellent, by the soul of my grandfather!" And the old Queen all the while kept saying, "Eat away, for you know what you eat." At first the King paid no attention to what she said; but at last, hearing the music continue, he replied, "Ay, I know well enough what I eat, for YOU brought nothing to the house." And at last, getting up in a rage, he went off to a villa at a little distance to cool his anger.

Meanwhile the Queen, not satisfied with what she had done, called the secretary again, and sent him to fetch Talia, pretending that the King wished to see her. At this summons Talia went that very instant, longing to see the light of her eyes, and not knowing that only the smoke awaited her. But when she

Glancing over her shoulder, she turned he key.

Told Again - Old Tales Told Again, 1927.

Illustrated by A. H. Watson.

came before the Queen, the latter said to her, with the face of a Nero, and full of poison as a viper, "Welcome, Madam Sly-cheat! Are you indeed the pretty mischief-maker? Are you the weed that has caught my son's eye and given me all this trouble."

When Talia heard this she began to excuse herself; but the Queen would not listen to a word; and having a large fire lighted in the courtyard, she commanded that Talia should be thrown into the flames. Poor Talia, seeing matters come to a bad pass, fell on her knees before the Queen, and besought her at least to grant her time to take the clothes from off her back. Whereupon the Queen, not so much out of pity for the unhappy girl, as to get possession of her dress, which was embroidered all over with gold and pearls, said to her, "Undress yourself—I allow you." Then Talia began to undress, and as she took off each garment she uttered an exclamation of grief; and when she had stripped off her cloak, her gown, and her jacket, and was proceeding to take off her petticoat, they seized her and were dragging her away. At that moment the King came up, and seeing the spectacle he demanded to know the whole truth; and when he asked also for the children, and heard that his stepmother had ordered them to be killed, the unhappy King gave himself up to despair.

He then ordered her to be thrown into the same fire which had been lighted for Talia, and the secretary with her, who was the handle of this cruel game and the weaver of this wicked web. Then he was going to do the same with the cook, thinking that he had killed the children; but the cook threw himself at the King's feet and said, "Truly, sir King, I would desire no other sinecure in return for the service I have done you than to be thrown into a furnace full of live coals; I would ask no other gratuity than the thrust of a spike; I would wish for no other amusement than to be roasted in the fire; I would desire no other privilege than to have the ashes of the cook mingled with those of a Queen. But I look for no such great reward for having saved the children, and brought them back to you in spite of that wicked creature who wished to kill them."

The Princess found her.

The Sleeping Beauty Picture Book, 1899.

Illustrated by Walter Crane

"I wish I could spin too," said the Princess. "Will you let me try?"
Fairy Tales, 1915.
Illustrated by Margaret Tarrant

When the King heard these words he was quite beside himself; he appeared to dream, and could not believe what his ears had heard. Then he said to the cook, "If it is true that you have saved the children, be assured I will take you from turning the spit, and reward you so that you shall call yourself the happiest man in the world."

As the King was speaking these words, the wife of the cook, seeing the dilemma her husband was in, brought Sun and Moon before the King, who, playing at the game of three with Talia and the other children, went round and round kissing first one and then another. Then giving the cook a large reward, he made him his chamberlain; and he took Talia to wife, who enjoyed a long life with her husband and the children, acknowledging that—

> "He who has luck may go to bed,
> And bliss will rain upon his head."

Let me see if I can do it.
The Tales of Mother Goose, 1901.
Illustrated by D. J. Munro

La Belle au Bois Dormant

(A French Tale)

La Belle au Bois Dormant was penned by Charles Perrault (1628-1703), a French author and member of the Académie Française – a man largely responsible for laying the foundations of the fairy-tale genre. It was published in 1697, in *Histoires ou Contes du Temps Passé: Les Contes de ma Mère l'Oye* ('Tales and Stories of the Past with Morals: Tales of Mother Goose'). All of Perrault's works were based on pre-existing stories, but his flair for storytelling 'fixed' the narrative as we know it today.

This particular tale borrows heavily from Giambattista Basile, and echoes its two-part story structure; the first section ending with the princess's discovery, and the second recounting her subsequent tribulations. The most notable differences in the plot are that, in Perrault's version, the sleep stems from a curse (instead of prophesised, as in the Basile and Ancient Egyptian tales), and the enchantment happens to end when the Prince arrives (as opposed to wakened when the child sucks on her finger, thereby removing the poisoned flax). Perrault was one of the last story-tellers to avoid waking the princess with a kiss.

There were formerly a King and a Queen, who were so sorry that they had no children, so sorry that it cannot be expressed. They went to all the waters in the world; vows, pilgrimages, all ways were tried and all to no purpose. At last, however, the Queen proved with child, and was brought to bed of a daughter. There was a very fine christening; and the Princess had for her godmothers all the Fairies they could find in the whole kingdom (they found seven), that every one of them might give her a gift, as was the custom of Fairies in those days, and that by this means the Princess might have all the perfections imaginable.

After the ceremonies of the christening were over, all the company returned to the King's palace, where was prepared a great feast for the Fairies. There was placed before every one of them a magnificent cover with a case of massive gold, wherein were a spoon, knife and fork, all of pure gold set with diamonds and rubies. But as they were all sitting down at table, they saw come into the hall a very old Fairy whom they had not invited, because it was above fifty years since she had been out of a certain tower, and she was believed to be either dead or enchanted. The King ordered her a cover, but could not furnish her with a case of gold as the others, because they had seven only made for the seven Fairies. The old Fairy fancied she was slighted, and muttered some threat between her teeth. One of the young Fairies, who sat by her, overheard how she grumbled; and judging that she might give the little Princess some unlucky gift, went, as soon as they rose from the table, and hid herself behind the hangings, that she might speak last, and repair, as much as possible she could, the evil which the old Fairy might intend.

In the mean while all the Fairies began to give their gifts to the Princess. The youngest gave her for gift, that she should be the most beautiful person in the world; the next, that she should have the wit of an angel; the third, that she should have a wonderful grace in every thing she did; the fourth, that she should dance perfectly well; the fifth, that she should sing like a nightingale; and the sixth, that she should play upon all kinds of music to the utmost perfection.

The old Fairy's turn coming next, with a head shaking more with spite than age, she said, that the Princess should have her hand pierced with a spindle, and die of the wound. This terrible gift made the whole company tremble, and every body fell a-crying.

Briar Rose.

Old, Old Fairy Tales, 1935.

Illustrated by Anne Anderson

How prettily that little thing turns round!
My Book of Favourite Fairy Tales, 1921.
Illustrated by Jennie Harbour

At this very instant the young Fairy came out from behind the hangings, and spake these words aloud:

"Be reassured, O King and Queen; your daughter shall not die of this disaster: it is true, I have no power to undo entirely what my elder has done. The Princess shall indeed pierce her hand with a spindle; but instead of dying, she shall only fall into a profound sleep, which shall last a hundred years; at the expiration of which a king's son shall come and awake her."

The King, to avoid the misfortune foretold by the old Fairy, caused immediately proclamations to be made, whereby every-body was forbidden, on pain of death, to spin with a distaff and spindle or to have so much as any spindle in their houses.

About fifteen or sixteen years after, the King and Queen being gone to one of their houses of pleasure, the young Princess happened one day to divert herself running up and down the palace; when going up from one apartment to another, she came into a little room on the top of a tower, where a good old woman, alone, was spinning with her spindle. This good woman had never heard of the King's proclamation against spindles.

"What are you doing there, Goody?" said the Princess.

"I am spinning, my pretty child," said the old woman, who did not know who she was.

"Ha!" said the Princess, "this is very pretty; how do you do it? Give it to me, that I may see if I can do so." She had no sooner taken the spindle into her hand, than, whether being very hasty at it, somewhat unhandy, or that the decree of the Fairy had so ordained it, it ran into her hand, and she fell down in a swoon.

The Sleeping Beauty.
Grimm's Fairy Tales, 1909.
Illustrated by Millicent Sowerby

The good old woman not knowing very well what to do in this affair, cried out for help. People came in from every quarter in great numbers; they threw water upon the Princess's face, unlaced her, struck her on the palms of her hands, and rubbed her temples with Hungary-water; but nothing would bring her to herself.

And now the King, who came up at the noise, bethought himself of the prediction of the Fairies, and judging very well that this must necessarily come to pass, since the Fairies had said it, caused the Princess to be carried into the finest apartment in his palace, and to be laid upon a bed all embroidered with gold and silver. One would have taken her for an angel, she was so very beautiful; for her swooning away had not diminished one bit of her complexion; her cheeks were carnation, and her lips like coral; indeed her eyes were shut, but she was heard to breathe softly, which satisfied those about her that she was not dead. The King commanded that they should not disturb her, but let her sleep quietly till her hour of awakening was come.

The good Fairy, who had saved her life by condemning her to sleep a hundred years, was in the kingdom of Matakin, twelve thousand leagues off, when this accident befell the Princess; but she was instantly informed of it by a little dwarf, who had boots of seven leagues, that is, boots with which he could tread over seven leagues of ground at one stride. The Fairy came away immediately, and she arrived, about an hour after, in a fiery chariot, drawn by dragons. The King handed her out of the chariot, and she approved every thing he had done; but, as she had a very great fore sight, she thought, when the Princess should awake, she might not know what to do with herself, being all alone in this old palace; and this was what she did: She touched with her wand every thing in the palace (except the King and the Queen), governesses, maids of honour, ladies of the bedchamber, gentlemen, officers, stewards, cooks, under-cooks, scullions, guards, with their beef-eaters, pages, footmen; she likewise touched all the horses which were in the stables, as well as their

She fell into a swoon.
Tales of Passed Times, 1900
Illustrated by Charles Robinson

grooms, the great dogs in the outward court, and pretty little Mopsey too, the Princess's little spaniel-bitch, which lay by her on the bed.

Immediately upon her touching them, they all fell asleep, that they might not awake before their mistress, and that they might be ready to wait upon her when she wanted them. The very spits at the fire, as full as they could hold of partridges and pheasants, did fall asleep, and the fire likewise. All this was done in a moment. Fairies are not long in doing their business.

And now the King and the Queen, having kissed their dear child without waking her, went out of the palace, and put forth a proclamation, that nobody should dare to come near it. This, however, was not necessary; for, in a quarter of an hour's time, there grew up, all round about the park, such a vast number of trees, great and small, bushes and brambles, twining one within another, that neither man nor beast could pass thro'; so that nothing could be seen but the very top of the towers of the palace; and that too, not unless it was a good way off. Nobody doubted but the Fairy gave herein a sample of her art, that the Princess, while she continued sleeping, might have nothing to fear from any curious people.

When a hundred years were gone and past, the son of the King then reigning, and who was of another family from that of the sleeping Princess, being gone a-hunting on that side of the country, asked, what were those towers which he saw in the middle of a great thick wood? Every one answered according as they had heard; some said that it was a ruinous old castle, haunted by spirits; others, that all the sorcerers and witches of the country kept there their sabbath, or nights meeting. The common opinion was that an Ogre lived there, and that he carried thither all the little children he could catch, that he might eat them up at his leisure, without any-body's being able to follow him, as having himself, only, the power to pass thro' the wood.

The Prince was at a stand, not knowing what to believe, when a very aged countryman spake to him thus: "May it please your Royal Highness, it is now above fifty years since I heard my father, who had heard my grandfather, say that there then was in this castle, a Princess, the most beautiful was ever seen; that she must sleep there a hundred years, and should be awaked by a king's son; for whom she was reserved." The young Prince was all on fire at these words, believing, without a moment's doubt, that he could put an end to this rare adventure; and pushed on by love and honour resolved that moment to look into it.

Scarce had he advanced towards the wood, when all the great trees, the bushes and brambles, gave way of themselves to let him pass thro'; he walked up to the castle which he saw at the end of a large avenue which he went into; and what a little surprised him was, that he saw none of his people could follow him, because the trees closed again, as soon as he had pass'd thro' them. However, he did not cease from continuing his way; a young and amorous Prince is always valiant. He came into a spacious outward court, where everything he saw might have frozen up the most fearless person with horror. There reigned over all a most frightful silence; the image of death everywhere shewed itself, and there was nothing to be seen but stretched out bodies of men and animals, all seeming to be dead. He, however, very well knew, by the ruby faces and pimpled noses of the beef-eaters, that they were only asleep; and their goblets, wherein still remained some drops of wine, shewed plainly, that they fell asleep in their cups.

He then crossed a court paved with marble, went up the stairs, and came into the guard-chamber, where the guards were standing in their ranks, with their muskets upon their shoulders, and snoring as loud as they could. After that he went through several rooms full of gentlemen and ladies, all asleep,

All they could do did not bring her to herself.
The Sleeping Beauty and Dick Whittington and His Cat, 1895.
Illustrated by R. Anning Bell

some standing, others sitting. At last he came into a chamber all gilded with gold, where he saw, upon a bed, the curtains of which were all open, the finest sight was ever beheld: a Princess, who appeared to be about fifteen or sixteen years of age, and whose bright, and in a manner resplendent beauty, had somewhat in it divine. He approached with trembling and admiration, and fell down before her upon his knees.

"He saw, upon a bed, the finest sight was ever beheld."

And now, as the enchantment was at an end, the Princess awaked, and looking on him with eyes more tender than the first view might seem to admit of: "Is it you, my Prince," said she to him, "you have tarried long."

The Prince, charmed with these words, and much more with the manner in which they were spoken, knew not how to shew his joy and gratitude; he assured her, that he loved her better than he did himself; his discourse was not well connected, but it pleased her all the more; little eloquence, a great deal of love. He was more at a loss than she, and we need not wonder at it; she had time to think on what to say to him; for it is very probable (though history mentions nothing of it) that the good Fairy, during so long a sleep, had entertained her with pleasant dreams. In short, when they talked four hours together, they said not half what they had to say.

In the mean while, all the palace awaked; every one thought upon their particular business; and as all of them were not in love, they were ready to die for hunger; the chief lady of honour, being as sharp set as other folks, grew very impatient, and told the Princess aloud, That supper was served up. The Prince helped the Princess to rise, she was entirely dressed, and very magnificently, but his Royal Highness took care not to tell her that she was dressed like his great grand-mother, and had a point-band peeping over a high collar; she looked not a bit the less beautiful and charming for all that.

They lay her on her bed.
The Sleeping Beauty Picture Book, 1899.
Illustrated by Walter Crane

The Sleeping Princess.
The Allies' Fairy Book, 1916.
Illustrated by Arthur Rackham

They went into the great hall of looking-glasses, where they supped, and were served by the Princess's officers; the violins and hautboys played old tunes, but very excellent, tho' it was now above a hundred years since they had been played; and after supper, without losing any time, the lord almoner married them in the chapel of the castle, and the chief lady of honour drew the curtains. They had but very little sleep; the Princess had no occasion, and the Prince left her next morning to return into the city, where his father must needs have been anxious on his account. The Prince told him that he lost his way in the forest, as he was hunting, and that he had lain at the cottage of a collier, who gave him cheese and brown bread.

The King his father, who was of an easy disposition, believed him; but his mother could not be persuaded this was true; and seeing that he went almost every day a-hunting, and that he always had some excuse ready when he had laid out three or four nights together, she no longer doubted he had some little amour, for he lived with the Princess above two whole years, and had by her two children, the eldest of which, who was a daughter, was named Aurora, and the youngest, who was a son, they called Day, because he was even handsomer and more beautiful than his sister.

The Queen said more than once to her son, in order to bring him to speak freely to her, that a young man must e'en take his pleasure; but he never dared to trust her with his secret; he feared her, tho' he loved her; for she was of the race of the Ogres, and the King would never have married her, had it not been for her vast riches; it was even whispered about the court, that she had Ogreish inclinations, and that, whenever she saw little children passing by, she had all the difficulty in the world to refrain from falling upon them. And so the Prince would never tell her one word.

But when the King was dead, which happened about two years afterwards; and he saw himself lord and master, he openly declared his marriage; and he went in great ceremony to fetch his Queen from the castle. They made a magnificent entry into the capital city, she riding between her two children.

Some time after, the King went to make war with the Emperor Cantalabutte, his neighbour. He left the government of the kingdom to the Queen his mother, and earnestly recommended to her care his wife and children. He was like to be at war all the summer, and as soon as he departed, the Queen-mother sent her daughter-in-law and her children to a country-house among the woods, that she might with the more ease gratify her horrible longing.

Some few days afterwards she went thither herself, and said to her clerk of the kitchen:

"I have a mind to eat little Aurora for my dinner to morrow."

"Ah! Madam," cried the clerk of the kitchen.

"I will have it so," replied the Queen (and this she spake in the tone of an Ogress, who had a strong desire to eat fresh meat), "and will eat her with a Sauce Robert."

The poor man knowing very well that he must not play tricks with Ogresses, took his great knife and went up into little Aurora's chamber. She was then four years old, and came up to him jumping and laughing, to take him about the neck, and ask him for some sugar-candy. Upon which he began to weep, the great knife fell out of his hand, and he went into the back-yard, and killed a little lamb, and dressed it with such good sauce, that his mistress assured him she had never eaten anything so good in her life. He had at the same time taken up little Aurora, and carried her to his wife, to conceal her in the lodging he had at the end of the court yard.

A little dwarf who had a pair of seven-league boots.
Old Time Stories, 1921.
Illustrated by W. Heath Robinson

She was not dead, but had only fallen into a deep sleep.
Grimm's Household Tales, 1912.
Illustrated by R. Anning Bell

About eight days afterwards, the wicked Queen said to the clerk of the kitchen:

"I will sup upon little Day."

He answered not a word, being resolved to cheat her, as he had done before. He went to find out little Day, and saw him with a little foil in his hand, with which he was fencing with a great monkey; the child being then only three years of age. He took him up in his arms, and carried him to his wife, that she might conceal him in her chamber along with his sister, and in the room of little Day cooked up a young kid very tender, which the Ogress found to be wonderfully good.

This was hitherto all mighty well: but one evening this wicked Queen said to her clerk of the kitchen:

"I will eat the Queen with the same sauce I had with her children."

It was now that the poor clerk of the kitchen despaired of being able to deceive her. The young Queen was turned of twenty, not reckoning the hundred years she had been asleep: her skin was somewhat tough, tho' very fair and white; and how to find in the yard a beast so firm, was what puzzled him. He took then a resolution, that he might save his own life, to cut the Queen's throat; and going up into her chamber, with intent to do it at once, he put himself into as great a fury as he could possibly, and came into the young Queen's room with his dagger in his hand. He would not, however, surprise her, but told her, with a great deal of respect, the orders he had received from the Queen-mother.

"Do it, do it," said she stretching out her neck, "execute your orders, and then I shall go and see my children, my poor children, whom I so much and so tenderly loved," for she thought them dead ever since they had been taken away without her knowledge.

"No, no, Madam," cried the poor clerk of the kitchen, all in tears, "you shall not die, and yet you shall see your children again; but it must be in my lodgings, where I have concealed them, and I shall deceive the Queen once more, by giving her in your stead a young hind."

Upon this he forthwith conducted her to his chamber; where leaving her to embrace her children, and cry along with them, he went and dressed a hind, which the Queen had for her supper, and devoured it with the same appetite, as if it had been the young Queen. Exceedingly was she delighted with her cruelty, and she had invented a story to tell the King, at his return, how ravenous wolves had eaten up the Queen his wife, and her two children.

One evening, as she was, according to her custom, rambling round about the courts and yards of the palace, to see if she could smell any fresh meat, she heard, in a ground-room little Day crying, for his mamma was going to whip him, because he had been naughty; and she heard, at the same time, little Aurora begging pardon for her brother.

The Ogress presently knew the voice of the Queen and her children, and being quite mad that she had been thus deceived, she commanded next morning, by break of day (with a most horrible voice, which made every body tremble) that they should bring into the middle of the great court a large tub, which she caused to be filled with toads, vipers, snakes, and all sorts of serpents, in order to have thrown into it the Queen and her children, the clerk of the kitchen, his wife and maid; all whom she had given orders should be brought thither with their hands tied behind them.

They all went to sleep also.
Perrault's Fairy Tales, 1913.
Illustrated by Honor Appleton

They were brought out accordingly, and the executioners were just going to throw them into the tub, when the King (who was not so soon expected) entered the court on horse-back (for he came post) and asked, with the utmost astonishment, what was the meaning of that horrible spectacle? No one dared to tell him; when the Ogress, all enraged to see what had happened, threw herself head-foremost into the tub, and was instantly devoured by the ugly creatures she had ordered to be thrown into it for others. The King could not but be very sorry, for she was his mother; but he soon comforted himself with his beautiful wife, and his pretty children.

The Moral

To get as prize a husband rich and gay.
Of humour sweet, with many years to stay,
Is natural enough, 'tis true;
To wait for him a hundred years,
And all that while asleep, appears
A thing entirely new.
Now at this time of day,
Not one of all the sex we see
Doth sleep with such profound tranquillity:
But yet this Fable seems to let us know
That very often Hymen's blisses sweet,
Altho' some tedious obstacles they meet,
Are not less happy for approaching slow.
'Tis nature's way that ladies fair
Should yearn conjugal joys to share;
And so I've not the heart to preach
A moral that's beyond their reach.

The King and Queen fall asleep.
The Big Book of Fairy Tales, 1911.
Illustrated by Charles Robinson

They grow until nothing but the tops of the castle towers could be seen.
The Sleeping Beauty and Other Fairy Tales From the Old French, 1910.
Illustrated by Edmund Dulac

DORNRÖNSCHEN

(A German Tale)

Dornrönschen ('Little Briar Rose') is a tale collected by the Brothers Grimm, (or *Die Brüder Grimm*), Jacob (1785–1863) and Wilhelm Grimm (1786–1859). It was first published in *Kinder und Hausmärchen* ('Children's and Household Tales') in 1812. *Kinder und Hausmärchen* was a pioneering collection of German folklore, and the Grimms built their anthology on the conviction that a national identity could be found in popular culture and with the common folk (*Volk*). Their first volumes were highly criticised however, because although they were called 'Children's Tales', they were not regarded as suitable for children, for both their scholarly information and gruesome subject matter.

Little Briar Rose appeared in the original handwritten version of the Grimm's Fairy Tales (1810), told to them by Marie Hassenpflug. Unlike the stories of Basile and Perrault, *Little Briar Rose* ends when the prince arrives to wake the fair maiden. The Brothers Grimm also included, in the first edition of their tales, a fragmentary addition; *The Evil Mother-in-Law.* This began with the heroine married and the mother of two children, as in the second part of Perrault's tale, with her mother-in-law attempting to eat first the children and then the heroine. Like many German tales showing French influence though, it appeared in no subsequent editions.

Come and gone a hundred years!
An Old Fairy Tale - The Sleeping Beauty, 1868.
Illustrated by The Dalziel Brothers

A long time ago there were a King and Queen who said every day, "Ah, if only we had a child!" but they never had one. But it happened that once when the Queen was bathing, a frog crept out of the water on to the land, and said to her, "Your wish shall be fulfilled; before a year has gone by, you shall have a daughter."

What the frog had said came true, and the Queen had a little girl who was so pretty that the King could not contain himself for joy, and ordered a great feast. He invited not only his kindred, friends and acquaintance, but also the Wise Women, in order that they might be kind and well-disposed towards the child. There were thirteen of them in his kingdom, but, as he had only twelve golden plates for them to eat out of, one of them had to be left at home.

The feast was held with all manner of splendour and when it came to an end the Wise Women bestowed their magic gifts upon the baby: one gave virtue, another beauty, a third riches, and so on with everything in the world that one can wish for.

When eleven of them had made their promises, suddenly the thirteenth came in. She wished to avenge herself for not having been invited, and without greeting, or even looking at any one, she cried with a loud voice, "The King's daughter shall in her fifteenth year prick herself with a spindle, and fall down dead." And, without saying a word more, she turned round and left the room.

They were all shocked; but the twelfth, whose good wish still remained unspoken, came forward, and as she could not undo the evil sentence, but only soften it, she said, "It shall not be death, but a deep sleep of a hundred years, into which the princess shall fall."

The King, who would fain keep his dear child from the misfortune, gave orders that every spindle in the whole kingdom should be burnt. Meanwhile the gifts of the Wise Women were plenteously fulfilled on the young girl, for she was so beautiful, modest, good-natured, and wise, that everyone who saw her was bound to love her.

It happened that on the very day when she was fifteen years old, the King and Queen were not at home, and the maiden was left in the palace quite alone. So she went round into all sorts of places, looked into rooms and bed-chambers just as she liked, and at last came to an old tower. She climbed up the narrow winding-staircase, and reached a little door. A rusty key was in the lock, and when she turned it the door sprang open, and there in a little room sat an old woman with a spindle, busily spinning her flax.

"Good day, old dame," said the King's daughter; "what are you doing there?" "I am spinning," said the old woman, and nodded her head. "What sort of thing is that, that rattles round so merrily?" said the girl, and she took the spindle and wanted to spin too. But scarcely had she touched the spindle when the magic decree was fulfilled, and she pricked her finger with it.

And, in the very moment when she felt the prick, she fell down upon the bed that stood there, and lay in a deep sleep. And this sleep extended over the whole palace; the King and Queen who had just come home, and had entered the great hall, began to go to sleep, and the whole of the court with them. The horses, too, went to sleep in the stable, the dogs in the yard, the pigeons upon the roof, the flies on the wall; even the fire that was flaming on the hearth became quiet and slept, the roast meat left off frizzling, and the cook, who was just going to pull the hair of the scullery boy, because he had forgotten something, let him go, and went to sleep. And the wind fell, and on the trees before the castle not a leaf moved again.

But round about the castle there began to grow a hedge of thorns, which every year became higher, and at last grew close up round the castle and all

The sharp thorns gripped the unhappy young men like clutching hands, and held them fast.
The Sleeping Beauty Told by C. S. Evans, 1920.
Illustrated by Arthur Rackham

over it, so that there was nothing of it to be seen, not even the flag upon the roof. But the story of the beautiful sleeping "Briar-rose," for so the princess was named, went about the country, so that from time to time kings' sons came and tried to get through the thorny hedge into the castle.

But they found it impossible, for the thorns held fast together, as if they had hands, and the youths were caught in them, could not get loose again, and died a miserable death.

After long, long years a King's son came again to that country, and heard an old man talking about the thorn-hedge, and that a castle was said to stand behind it in which a wonderfully beautiful princess, named Briar-rose, had been asleep for a hundred years; and that the King and Queen and the whole court were asleep likewise. He had heard, too, from his grandfather, that many kings' sons had already come, and had tried to get through the thorny hedge, but they had remained sticking fast in it, and had died a pitiful death. Then the youth said, "I am not afraid, I will go and see the beautiful Briar-rose." The good old man might dissuade him as he would, he did not listen to his words.

But by this time the hundred years had just passed, and the day had come when Briar-rose was to awake again. When the King's son came near to the thorn-hedge, it was nothing but large and beautiful flowers, which parted from each other of their own accord, and let him pass unhurt, then they closed again behind him like a hedge. In the castle-yard he saw the horses and the spotted hounds lying asleep; on the roof sat the pigeons with their heads under their wings. And when he entered the house, the flies were asleep upon the wall, the cook in the kitchen was still holding out his hand to seize the boy, and the maid was sitting by the black hen which she was going to pluck.

He went on farther, and in the great hall he saw the whole of the court lying asleep, and up by the throne lay the King and Queen.

There they stuck fast and died miserably.
My Book of Favourite Fairy Tales, 1921.
Illustrated by Jennie Harbour

Hound and huntsman have followed fast.
An Old Fairy Tale - The Sleeping Beauty, 1868.
Illustrated by The Dalziel Brothers

Then he went on still farther, and all was so quiet that a breath could be heard, and at last he came to the tower, and opened the door into the little room where Briar-rose was sleeping. There she lay, so beautiful that he could not turn his eyes away; and he stooped down and gave her a kiss. But as soon as he kissed her, Briar-rose opened her eyes and awoke, and looked at him quite sweetly.

Then they went down together, and the King awoke, and the Queen, and the whole court, and looked at each other in great astonishment. And the horses in the court-yard stood up and shook themselves; the hounds jumped up and wagged their tails; the pigeons upon the roof pulled out their heads from under their wings, looked round, and flew into the open country; the flies on the wall crept again; the fire in the kitchen burned up and flickered and cooked the meat; the joint began to turn and frizzle again, and the cook gave the boy such a box on the ear that he screamed, and the maid plucked the fowl ready for the spit.

And then the marriage of the King's son with Briar-rose was celebrated with all splendour, and they lived contented to the end of their days.

The Prince enquires of the aged countryman.
The Fairy Tales of Charles Perrault, 1922.
Illustrated by Harry Clarke

LITTLE SURYA BAI

(An Indian Tale)

This tale was first translated into English by Mary Eliza Isabella Frere (1845 - 1911), a British author who published many works to do with the Indian continent. Frere's book, *Old Deccan Days; or, Hindoo Fairy Legends Current in Southern India. Collected From Oral Tradition* (1868), was the first English-language field-collection of Indian chronicles. According to Frere's introduction, she began her collection during long travels with her father.

Frere's anthology was highly influential, and in a review by the German orientologist Max Müller, was praised for its rendition of Sanskrit reading 'like a direct translation of the ancient language.' In this variant on the *Sleeping Beauty* narrative, Surya Bai (meaning 'The Sun Lady') is caused to fall into her sleep by a splinter coming out of the wall of an Eagle's cage. She is thereafter rescued and married by a Rajah. The evil step-mother is also replaced in this version, by a jealous and competing wife.

➤———→

A poor Milkwoman was once going into the town with cans full of milk to sell. She took with her her little daughter (a baby of about a year old), having no one in whose charge to leave her at home. Being tired, she sat down by the roadside, placing the child and the cans full of milk beside her; when, on a sudden, two large Eagles flew overhead, and one, swooping down, seized the child, and flew away with her out of the mother's sight.

73

An aged peasant told of an enchanted palace.
The Sleeping Beauty Picture Book, 1899.
Illustrated by Walter Crane

Very far, far away the Eagle carried the little baby; even beyond the borders of her native land, until they reached their home in a lofty tree. There the old Eagles had built a great nest; it was made of iron and wood, and was as big as a little house; there was iron all round, and to get in and out you had to go through seven iron doors.

In this stronghold they placed the little baby, and because she was like a young Eaglet they called her Surya Bai (The Sun Lady). The Eagles both loved the child; and daily they flew into distant countries to bring her rich and precious things. Clothes that had been made for princesses, precious jewels, wonderful playthings, all that was most costly and rare.

One day, when Surya Bai was twelve years old, the old husband Eagle said to his wife; 'Wife, our daughter has no diamond ring on her little finger, such as princesses wear; let us go and fetch her one.' 'Yes,' said the other old Eagle; 'but to fetch it we must go very far.' 'True,' rejoined he, 'such a ring is not to be got nearer than the Red Sea, and that is a twelve month's journey from here; nevertheless we will go.' So the Eagles started off, leaving Surya Bai in the strong nest, with twelve months' provisions (that she might not be hungry whilst they were away), and a little dog and cat to take care of her.

Some time after they were gone, one day the naughty little cat stole some food from the store, for doing which Surya Bai punished her. The cat did not like being whipped, and she was still more annoyed at having been caught stealing; so, in revenge, she ran to the fireplace (they were obliged to keep a fire always burning in the Eagles' nest, as Surya Bai never went down from the tree, and would not otherwise have been able to cook her dinner), and put out the fire. When the little girl saw this, she was much vexed, for the cat had eaten their last cooked provisions, and she did not know what they were to do for food. For three whole days Surya Bai puzzled over the difficulty, and for three whole days she, and the dog, and the cat, had nothing to eat. At last she thought she would climb to the edge of the nest, and see if she could see any fire in the country below; and, if so, she would go down and ask the people who lighted it to give her a little with which to cook her dinner. So she climbed to the edge of the nest. Then, very far away on the horizon, she saw a thin curl of blue smoke. So she let herself down from the tree, and all day long she walked in the direction whence the smoke came. Towards evening she reached the place, and found it rose from a small hut in which sat an old woman warming her hands over a fire. Now, though Surya Bai did not know it, she had reached the Rakshas' country, and this old woman was none other than a wicked old Rakshas, who lived with her son in the little hut. The young Rakshas, however, had gone out for the day. When the old Rakshas saw Surya Bai, she was much astonished, for the girl was beautiful as the Sun, and her rich dress was resplendent with jewels; and she said to herself, 'How lovely this child is! what a dainty morsel she would be! Oh, if my son were only here we would kill her, and boil her, and eat her. I will try and detain her till his return.'

Then turning to Surya Bai, she said, 'Who are you, and what do you want?' Surya Bai answered, 'I am the daughter of the great Eagles, but they have gone a far journey to fetch me a diamond ring, and the fire has died out in the nest. Give me, I pray you, a little from your hearth.' The Rakshas replied, 'You shall certainly have some, only first pound this rice for me, for I am old, and have no daughter to help me.' Then Surya Bai pounded the rice, but the young Rakshas had not returned by the time she had finished; so the old Rakshas said to her, 'If you are kind, grind this corn for me, for it is hard work for my old hands.' Then she ground the corn, but still the young Rakshas came not; and the old Rakshas said to her, 'Sweep the house for me first, and then I will give you the fire.' So Surya Bai swept the house; but still the young Rakshas did not come.

Then his mother said to Surya Bai, 'Why should you be in such a hurry to go home? Fetch me some water from the well and then you shall have the fire.'

*The young Prince said, 'I am not afraid; I am determined
to go and look upon the lovely Briar Rose.'*

The Fairy Tales of the Brothers Grimm, 1909.

Illustrated by Arthur Rackham

With loud hurrahs they cheered him up.
An Old Fairy Tale - The Sleeping Beauty, 1868.
Illustrated by The Dalziel Brothers

And she fetched the water. When she had done so, Surya Bai said, 'I have done all your bidding; now give me the fire, or I will go elsewhere and seek it.'

The old Rakshas was grieved because her son had not returned home: but she saw she could detain Surya Bai no longer, so she said, 'Take the fire and go in peace; take also some parched corn, and scatter it along the road as you go, so as to make a pretty little pathway from our house to yours;' and so saying she gave Surya Bai several handfuls of parched corn. The girl took them, fearing no evil, and as she went she scattered the grains on the road. Then she climbed back into the nest and shut the seven iron doors, and lighted the fire, and cooked the food, and gave the dog and the cat some dinner, and took some herself, and went to sleep.

Scarcely had Surya Bai left the Rakshas' hut, when the young Rakshas returned, and his mother said to him, 'Alas, alas, my son! why did not you come sooner? Such a sweet little lamb has been here, and now we have lost her.' Then she told him all about Surya Bai. 'Which way did she go?' asked the young Rakshas; 'only tell me that, and I'll have her before morning.'

His mother had told him how she had given Surya Bai the parched corn to scatter on the road; and when he heard that, he followed up the track, and ran, and ran, and ran, till he came to the foot of the tree.

There, looking up, he saw the nest high in the branches above him.

Quick as thought, up he climbed, and reached the great outer door; and he shook it, and shook it, but he could not get in, for Surya Bai had bolted it. Then he said, 'Let me in, my child, let me in; I'm the great Eagle, and I have come from very far, and brought you many beautiful jewels; and here is a splendid diamond ring to fit your little finger.' But Surya Bal did not hear him, she was fast asleep.

He next tried to force open the door again, but it was too strong for him. In his efforts, however, he had broken off one of his finger-nails--(now the nail of a Rakshas is most poisonous)--which he left sticking in the crack of the door when he went away.

Next morning Surya Bai opened all the doors in order to look down on the world below; but when she came to the seventh door a sharp thing, which was sticking in it, ran into her hand, and immediately she fell down dead.

At that same moment the two poor old Eagles returned from their long twelvemonth's journey, bringing a beautiful diamond ring, which they had fetched for their little favourite from the Red Sea.

There she lay on the threshold of the nest, beautiful as ever, but cold and dead.

The Eagles could not bear the sight; so they placed the ring on her finger, and then, with loud cries, flew off to return no more.

But a little while after there chanced to come by a great Rajah, who was out on a hunting expedition. He came with hawks, and hounds, and attendants, and horses, and pitched his camp under the tree in which the Eagles' nest was built. Then looking up he saw, amongst the topmost branches, what appeared like a queer little house, and he sent some of his attendants to see what it was. They soon returned, and told the Rajah that up in the tree was a curious thing like a cage, having seven iron doors, and that on the threshold of the first door lay a fair maiden, richly dressed; that she was dead, and that beside her stood a little dog and a little cat.

There before him was a tangled hedge of thorne.
The Sleeping Beauty Told by C. S. Evans, 1920.
Illustrated by Arthur Rackham

When the prince approached the thorn hedge to him it was nothing but beautiful flowers which offered no resistance to his progress.

Grimm's Fairy Tales, 1911.

Illustrated by Charles Folkard

At this the Rajah commanded that they should be fetched down, and when he saw Surya Bai he felt very sad to think that she was dead. And he took her hand to feel if it were already stiff; but all her limbs were supple, nor had she become cold, as the dead are cold; and, looking again at her hand, the Rajah saw that a sharp thing, like a long thorn, had run into the tender palm, almost far enough to pierce through to the back of her hand.

He pulled it out, and no sooner had he done so than Surya Bai opened her eyes, and stood up, crying, 'Where am I? and who are you? Is it a dream, or true?'

The Rajah answered, 'It is all true, beautiful lady. I am Rajah of a neighbouring land; pray tell me who are you?'

She replied, 'I am the Eagles' child.' But he laughed: 'Nay he said, 'that cannot be, you are some great Princess.' 'No,' she answered, 'I am no royal lady; what I say is true. I have lived all my life in this tree. I am only the Eagles' child.'

Then the Rajah said, 'If you are not a Princess born, I will make you one; say only that you will be my Queen.'

Surya Bai consented, and the Rajah took her to his kingdom and made her his Queen. But Surya Bai was not his only wife and the first Ranee, his other wife, was both envious and jealot of her.

The Rajah gave Surya Bai many trustworthy attendants I guard her and be with her, and one old woman loved her more than all the rest, and used to say to her--' Don't be too intimate with the first Ranee, dear lady, for she wishes you no good, an she has power to do you harm. Some day she may poison or otherwise injure you.' But Surya Bai would answer he 'Nonsense! what is there to be alarmed about? Why cannot we both live happily together like two sisters?' Then the old woman would rejoin, 'Ah, dear lady, may you never live to rue your confidence! I pray my fears may prove folly.' So Surya Bai went often to see the first Ranee, and the first Ranee also came often to see her.

One day they were standing in the palace court-yard, near tank, where the Rajah's people used to bathe, and the first Ram said to Surya Bai, 'What pretty jewels you have, sister! let me try them on for a minute, and see how I look in them.'

The old woman was standing beside Surya Bai, and sh whispered to her, 'Do not lend your jewels.' 'Hush, you silly old woman,' answered she; 'what harm will it do?' and she gave the Ranee her jewels. Then the Ranee said, 'How pretty a your things are! do you not think they look well even on me Let us come down to the tank, it is as clear as glass, and we ca see ourselves reflected in it, and how these jewels will shine in the clear water!'

The old woman, hearing this, was much alarmed, and begged Surya Bai not to venture near the tank, but she said, 'I bid you be silent, I will not distrust my sister;' and she went down to the tank. Then, when no one was near, and they were both leaning over, looking at their reflections in the water, the first Ranee pushed Surya Bai into the tank, who, sinking under the water, was drowned; and from the place where her body fell there sprang up a bright golden sunflower.

The Rajah shortly afterwards inquired where Surya Bai was,--but nowhere could she be found. Then, very angry, he came to the first Ranee and said, 'Tell me where the child is. You have made away with her.' But she answered, 'You do me wrong, I know nothing of her. Doubtless that old woman, whom you allowed to be always with her, has done her some harm.' So the Rajah ordered the poor old woman to be thrown into prison.

He made his way over the rotting drawbridge, and went into the castle.
Told Again - Old Tales Told Again, 1927.
Illustrated by A. H. Watson

The Prince enters the silent palace.
The Sleeping Beauty, 1912.
Illustrated by John Hassall

He tried to forget Surya Bai and all her pretty ways, but it was no good. Wherever he went, he saw her face. Whatever he heard, he still listened for her voice. Every day he grew more miserable; he would not eat nor drink; and as for the other Ranee, he could not bear to speak to her. All his people said, 'He will surely die.'

When matters were in this state, the Rajah one day wandered to the edge of the tank, and bending over the parapet, looked into the water. Then he was surprised to see, growing out of the tank, close beside him, a stately golden flower; and as he watched it, the sunflower gently bent its head, and leaned down towards him. The Rajah's heart was softened, and he kissed its leaves and murmured, 'This flower reminds me of my lost wife. I love it, it is fair and gentle as she used to be.' And every day he would go down to the tank, and sit and watch the flower. When the Ranee heard this, she ordered her servants to go and dig up the sunflower, and to take it far into the jungle and burn it. Next time the Rajah went to the tank he found his flower gone, and he was very grieved, but none dared say who had done it.

Then, in the jungle, from the place where the ashes of the sunflower had been thrown, there sprang up a young mango tree, tall and straight, that grew so quickly, and became such a beautiful tree, that it was the wonder of all the country round. At last, on its topmost bough, came one fair blossom; and the blossom fell, and the little mango grew rosier and rosier, and larger and larger, till so wonderful was it, both for size and shape, that people flocked from far and near only to look at it.

But none ventured to gather it, for it was to be kept for the Rajah himself.

Now one day, the poor Milkwoman, Surya Bal's mother, was returning homewards after her day's work, with the empty milk. cans; and, being very tired with her long walk to the bazaar~ she lay down under the mango tree and fell asleep. Then right into her largest milk-can fell the wonderful mango. When the poor woman awoke and saw what had happened, she was dreadfully frightened, and thought to herself, 'If any one sees me with this wonderful fruit, that all the Rajah's great people have been watching for so many, many weeks, they will never believe that I did not steal it, and I shall be put in prison. Yet it is no good leaving it here; besides, it fell off of itself into my milk-can. I will therefore take it home as secretly as possible, and share it with my children.'

So the Milkwoman covered up the can in which the mango was, and took it quickly to her home, where she placed it in the corner of the room, and put over it a dozen other milk-cans, piled one above another. Then as soon as it was dark, she called her husband and eldest son (for she had six or seven children), and said to them, 'What good fortune do you think has befallen me to-day?'

'We cannot guess,' they said. 'Nothing less,' she when on, 'than the wonderful, wonderful mango falling into one of my milk-cans while I slept! I have brought it home with me; it is in that lowest can. Go, husband, call all the children to have a slice; and you, my son, take down that pile of cans, and fetch me the mango.' 'Mother,' he said, when he got to the lowest can, 'you were joking, I suppose, when you told us there was a mango here.'

'No, not at all,' she answered, 'there is a mango there. I put it there myself an hour ago.'

'Well, there's something quite different now,' replied her son. 'Come and see.'

The Milkwoman ran to the place, and there, in the lowest can, she saw, not the mango, but a little tiny wee lady, richly dressed in red and gold, and no bigger than a mango! On her head shone a bright jewel like a little sun.

All was so quiet that he could hear every breath he drew.
My Book of Favourite Fairy Tales, 1921.
Illustrated by Jennie Harbour

He could see the gold fish beneath the water-lily leaves lying still.
The Sleeping Beauty, 1920.
Illustrated by Arthur Rackham

'This is very odd,' said the mother. 'I never heard of such a thing in my life! But since she has been sent to us, I will take care of her as if she were my own child.'

Every day the little lady grew taller and taller, until she was the size of an ordinary woman; she was gentle and loveable, but always very sad and quiet, and she said her name was 'Surya Bai.'

The children were all very curious to know her history, but the Milk-woman and her husband would not let her be teased to say who she was, and said to the children, 'Let us wait. By and by, when she knows us better, she will most likely tell us her story of her own accord.'

Now it came to pass that once, when Surya Bai was taking water from the well for the old Milk-woman, the Rajah rode by, and as he saw her walking along, he cried, 'That is my wife,' and rode after her as fast as possible. Surya Bai, hearing a great clatter of horses' hoofs, was frightened, and ran home as quickly as she could, and hid herself; and when the Rajah reached the place there was only the old Milk-woman to be seen, standing at the door of her hut.

Then the Rajah said to her, 'Give her up, old woman, you have no right to keep her; she is mine, she is mine!' But the old woman answered, 'Are you mad? I don't know what you mean.'

The Rajah replied, 'Do not attempt to deceive me. I saw my wife go in at your door she must be in the house.'

'Your wife?' screamed the old woman--'your wife? You mean my daughter, who lately returned from the well! Do you think I am going to give up my child at your command? You are Rajah in your palace, but I am Rajah in my own house; and I won't give up my little daughter for any bidding of yours. Be off with you, or I'll pull out your beard.' And so saying she seized a long stick and attacked the Rajah, calling out loudly for assistance to her husband and sons, who came running to her aid.

The Rajah, seeing matters were against him, and having out-ridden his attendants (and not being quite certain moreover whether he had seen Surya Bai, or whether she might not have been really the poor Milk-woman's daughter), rode off and returned to his palace.

He determined, however, to sift the matter. As a first step he went to see Surya Bai's old attendant, who was still in prison. From her he learnt enough to make him believe she was not only entirely innocent of Surya Bai's death, but gravely to suspect the first Ranee of having caused it. He therefore ordered the old woman to be set at liberty--still keeping a watchful eye on her--and bade her prove her devotion to her long-lost mistress by going to the Milk-woman's house, and bringing him as much information as possible about the family, and more particularly about the girl he had seen returning from the well.

So the attendant went to the Milk-woman's house, and made friends with her, and bought some milk, and afterwards she stayed and talked to her.

This she did several times, and after a few days the Milkwoman ceased to be suspicious of her, and became quite cordial.

Surya Bai's attendant then told how she had been the late Ranee's waiting-woman, and how the Rajah had thrown her into prison on her mistress's death; in return for which intelligence the old Milk-woman imparted to her how the wonderful mango had tumbled into her can, as she slept under the tree; and how it had miraculously changed in the course of an hour into a beautiful little lady. 'I wonder why she should have chosen my poor house to live in, instead of any one else's,' said the old woman.

For a while he could see nothing.
Told Again - Old Tales Told Again, 1927.
Illustrated by A. H. Watson

Then Surya Bai's attendant said, 'Have you ever asked her her history? Perhaps she would not mind telling it to you now.'

So the Milk-woman called the girl, and as soon as the old attendant saw her, she knew it was none other than Surya Bai, and her heart jumped for joy; but she remained silent, wondering much, for she knew her mistress had been drowned in the tank.

The old Milk-woman turned to Surya Bai and said, 'My child, you have lived long with us, and been a good daughter to me; but I have never asked you your history, because I thought it must be a sad one; but if you do not fear to tell it to me now, I should like to hear it.'

Surya Bai answered, 'Mother, you speak true; my story is sad. I believe my real mother was a poor Milk-woman like you, and that she took me with her one day when I was quite a little baby, as she was going to sell milk in the bazaar. But being tired with the long walk, she sat down to rest, and placed me also on the ground, when suddenly a great Eagle flew down and carried me away. But all the father and mother I ever knew were the two great Eagles.'

'Ah, my child! my child!' cried the Milk-woman, 'I was that poor woman; the Eagles flew away with my eldest girl when she was only a year old. Have I found you after these many years!'

And she ran and called her children and husband, to tell them the wonderful news.

Then was there great rejoicing among them all.

La Belle Au Bois Dormant.
Contes De Fees, 1908.
Illustrated by Beauge Bertall

The King's son pressed on, into an inner chamber fair.
The Sleeping Beauty Picture Book, 1899.
Illustrated by Walter Crane

When they were a little calmer, her mother said to Surya Bai, 'Tell us, dear daughter, how your life has been spent since first we lost you.' And Surya Bai went on--

'The old Eagles took me away to their home, and there I lived happily many years. They loved to bring me all the most beautiful things they could find, and at last one day they both went to fetch me a diamond ring from the Red Sea; but while they were gone, the fire went out in the nest: so I went to an old woman's hut, and got her to give me some fire; and next day (I don't know how it was), as I was opening the outer door of the cage, a sharp thing that was sticking in it ran into my hand, and I fell down senseless.

'I don't know how long I lay there, but when I came to myself I found the Eagles must have come back, and thought me dead, and gone away, for the diamond ring was on my little finger; a great many people were watching over me, and amongst them wasa Rajah, who asked me to go home with him and be his wife, and he brought me to this place, and I was his Ranee...'

'But his other wife, the first Ranee, hated me (for she was jealous), and desired to kill me; and one day she accomplished her purpose, by pushing me into the tank, for I was young and foolish, and disregarded the warnings of my faithful old attendant, who begged me not to go near the place. Ah! if I had only listened to her words I might have been happy still.'

At this the old attendant, who had been sitting in the background, rushed forward and kissed Surya Bai's feet, crying, 'Ah, my lady! My lady! Have I found you at last?' And, without staying to hear more, she ran back to the Palace to tell the Rajah the glad news.

The most beautiful sight he had ever seen.
Old Time Stories, 1921.
Illustrated by W. Heath Robinson

Then Surya Bai told her parents how she had not wholly died in the tank, but become a sunflower; and how the first Ranee, seeing the Rajah's fondness for the plant, had caused it to be thrown away; and then how she had risen from the ashes of the sunflower in the form of a mango tree; and how when the tree blossomed all her spirit went into the little mango flower; and she ended by saying, 'And when the flower became fruit, I know not by what irresistible impulse I was induced to throw myself into your milk-can, mother. It was my destiny, and as soon as you took me into your house, I began to recover my human form.'

'Why, then,' asked her brothers and sisters, 'do you not tell the Rajah that you are living, and that you are the Ranee Surya Bai?'

'Alas!' she answered, 'I could not do that. Who knows but that he may now be influenced by the first Ranee, and desire my death? Let me rather be poor like you, but safe from danger.'

Then her mother cried, 'Oh, what a stupid woman I am! The Rajah one day came here seeking you, but I and your father and brothers drove him away, for we did not know you were indeed the lost Ranee.'

As she spoke these words a sound of horses' hoofs was heard in the distance, and the Rajah himself appeared, having learnt the good news of Surya Bai's being alive from her old attendant.

It is impossible to describe the joy of the Rajah at finding his long-lost wife, but it was not greater than Surya Bal's at being restored to her husband.

Then the Rajah turned to the old Milk-woman and said, 'Old woman, you did not tell me true, for it was indeed my wife who was in your hut'--'Yes, Protector of the poor,' answered the old Milk-woman, 'but it was also my daughter.' Then they told him how Surya Bai was the Milk-woman's child.

At hearing this the Rajah commanded them all to return with him to the Palace. He gave Surya Bai's father a village, and ennobled the family; and he said to Surya Bai's old attendant, 'For the good service you have done, you shall be Palace housekeeper;' and he gave her great riches, adding, 'I can never repay the debt I owe you, nor make you sufficient recompence for having caused you to be unjustly cast into prison.' But she replied, 'Sire, even in your anger you were temperate; if you had caused me to be put to death, as some would have done, none of this good might have come upon you; it is yourself you have to thank.'

The wicked first Ranee was cast, for the rest of her life, into the prison in which the old attendant had been thrown; but Surya Bai lived happily with her husband the rest of her days; and in memory of her adventures, he planted round their Palace a hedge of sunflowers and a grove of mango trees.

A young girl of wonderful beauty lay asleep on an embroidered bed.
The Fairy Book, 1923.
Illustrated by Warwick Goble

She lay fast asleep, and looked so beautiful that he could not turn his eyes away.
My Book of Favourite Fairy Tales, 1921.
Illustrated by Jennie Harbour

The King of England and His Three Sons

(An English Tale)

This story was written down by Joseph Jacobs (1854 - 1916), in his *More English Fairy Tales* (published in 1894). Jacobs was inspired by the work of the Brothers Grimm and the romantic nationalism common to folklorists of his age; he wished for English children to have access to English fairy tales, whereas they were chiefly reading French and German stories. In his own words, 'What Perrault began, the Grimms completed.'

Despite the 'sleeping beauty' format being of Italian, Icelandic or even of Egyptian Origin, the tale of *The King of England and His Three Sons* made it into the collection, as Jacobs discovered it in a book titled *In Gypsy Tents* (1880), where the informant was John Roberts, a Welsh gypsy. This narrative is not a traditional 'sleeping beauty' story, although the sleeping princess does provide the culmination of the narrative action. Instead of the princess being rescued by a prince, and taken back to his kingdom – in this story, it is the princess who goes in search of her suitor.

Once upon a time there was an old king who had three sons; and the old king fell very sick one time and there was nothing at all could make him well but some golden apples from a far country. So the three brothers went on horseback to look for some of these apples. They set off together, and when they came to cross-roads they halted and refreshed themselves a bit; and then they agreed to meet on a certain time, and not one was to go home before the other. So Valentine took the right, and Oliver went straight on, and poor Jack took the left.

To make my long story short, I shall follow poor Jack, and let the other two take their chance, for I don't think there was much good in them. Off poor Jack rides over hills, dales, valleys, and mountains, through woolly woods and sheepwalks, where the old chap never sounded his hollow bugle-horn, farther than I can tell you to-night or ever intend to tell you.

At last he came to an old house, near a great forest, and there was an old man sitting out by the door, and his look was enough to frighten you or any one else; and the old man said to him:

"Good morning, my king's son."

"Good morning to you, old gentleman," was the young prince's answer; frightened out of his wits though he was, he didn't like to give in.

The old gentleman told him to dismount and to go in to have some refreshment, and to put his horse in the stable, such as it was. Jack soon felt much better after having something to eat, and began to ask the old gentleman how he knew he was a king's son.

"Oh dear!" said the old man, "I knew that you were a king's son, and I know what is your business better than what you do yourself. So you will have to stay here to-night; and when you are in bed you mustn't be frightened whatever you may hear. There will come all manner of frogs and snakes, and some will try to get into your eyes and your mouth, but mind, don't stir the least bit or you will turn into one of those things yourself."

The Sleeping Beauty.
Four and Twenty Fairy Tales, 1858
Illustrated by Edward Corbould

Poor Jack didn't know what to make of this, but, however, he ventured to go to bed. Just as he thought to have a bit of sleep, round and over and under him they came, but he never stirred an inch all night.

"Well, my young son, how are you this morning?"

"Oh, I am very well, thank you, but I didn't have much rest."

"Well, never mind that; you have got on very well so far, but you have a great deal to go through before you can have the golden apples to go to your father. You'd better come and have some breakfast before you start on your way to my other brother's house. You will have to leave your own horse here with me until you come back again, and tell me everything about how you get on."

After that out came a fresh horse for the young prince, and the old man gave him a ball of yarn, and he flung it between the horse's two ears.

Off he went as fast as the wind, which the wind behind could not catch the wind before, until he came to the second oldest brother's house. When he rode up to the door he had the same salute as from the first old man, but this one was even uglier than the first one. He had long grey hair, and his teeth were curling out of his mouth, and his finger- and toe-nails had not been cut for many thousand years. He put the horse into a much better stable, and called Jack in, and gave him plenty to eat and drink, and they had a bit of a chat before they went to bed.

"Well, my young son," said the old man, "I suppose you are one of the king's children come to look for the golden apples to bring him back to health."

"Yes, I am the youngest of the three brothers, and I should like to get them to go back with."

The Prince brushed aside the curtains, and there, on a couch in the centre of a splendid room, lay the Princess, looking as if she had gone to sleep but an hour before.

Fairy Tales, 1915.

Illustrated by Margaret Tarrant

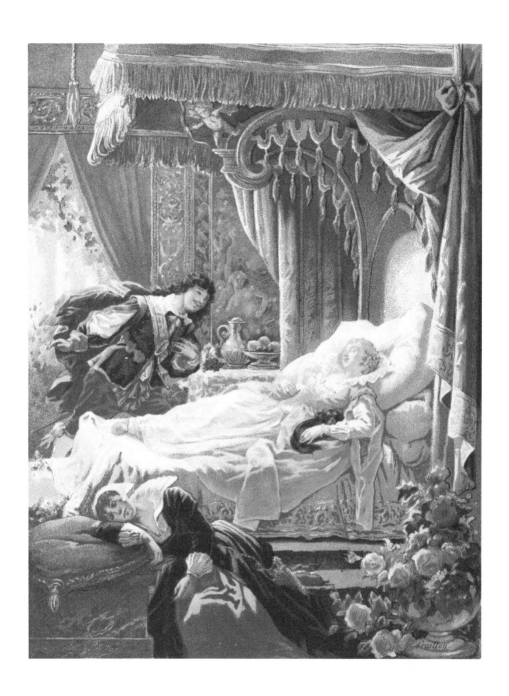

La Belle Au Bois Dormant.
Contes de Perrault, 1890.
Illustrated by Frédéric Théodore Lix

"Well, don't mind, my young son. Before you go to bed to-night I will send to my eldest brother, and will tell him what you want, and he won't have much trouble in sending you on to the place where you must get the apples. But mind not to stir to-night no matter how you get bitten and stung, or else you will work great mischief to yourself."

The young man went to bed and bore all, as he did the first night, and got up the next morning well and hearty. After a good breakfast out comes a fresh horse, and a ball of yarn to throw between his ears. The old man told him to jump up quick, and said that he had made it all right with his eldest brother, not to delay for anything whatever, "For," said he, "you have a good deal to go through with in a very short and quick time."

He flung the ball, and off he goes as quick as lightning, and comes to the eldest brother's house. The old man receives him very kindly and told him he long wished to see him, and that he would go through his work like a man and come back safe and sound. "To-night," said he, "I will give you rest; there shall nothing come to disturb you, so that you may not feel sleepy for to-morrow. And you must mind to get up middling early, for you've got to go and come all in the same day; there will be no place for you to rest within thousands of miles of that place; and if there was, you would stand in great danger never to come from there in your own form. Now, my young prince, mind what I tell you. To-morrow, when you come in sight of a very large castle, which will be surrounded with black water, the first thing you will do you will tie your horse to a tree, and you will see three beautiful swans in sight, and you will say, 'Swan, swan, carry me over in the name of the Griffin of the Greenwood,' and the swans will swim you over to the earth. There will be three great entrances, the first guarded by four great giants with drawn swords in their hands, the second by lions, the other by fiery serpents and dragons. You will have to be there exactly at one o'clock; and mind and leave there precisely at two and not a moment later. When the swans carry you over to the castle, you will pass all these things, all fast asleep, but you must not notice any of them.

"When you go in, you will turn up to the right; you will see some grand rooms, then you will go downstairs through the cooking kitchen, and through; a door on your left you go into a garden, where you will find the apples you want for your father to get well. After you fill your wallet, you make all speed you possibly can, and call out for the swans to carry you over the same as before. After you get on your horse, should you hear anything shouting or making any noise after you, be sure not to look back, as they will follow you for thousands of miles; but when the time is up and you get near my place, it will be all over. Well now, my young man, I have told you all you have to do to-morrow; and mind, whatever you do, don't look about you when you see all those frightful things asleep. Keep a good heart, and make haste from there, and come back to me with all the speed you can. I should like to know how my two brothers were when you left them, and what they said to you about me."

"Well, to tell the truth, before I left London my father was sick, and said I was to come here to look for the golden apples, for they were the only things that would do him good; and when I came to your youngest brother, he told me many things I had to do before I came here. And I thought once that your youngest brother put me in the wrong bed, when he put all those snakes to bite me all night long, until your second brother told me 'So it was to be,' and said, 'It is the same here,' but said you had none in your beds."

"Well, let's go to bed. You need not fear. There are no snakes here."

The young man went to bed, and had a good night's rest, and got up the next morning as fresh as newly caught trout. Breakfast being over, out comes the other horse, and, while saddling and fettling, the old man began to laugh, and told the young gentleman that if he saw a pretty young lady, not to stay with her too long, because she might waken, and then he would have to stay

The Sleeping Beauty.
A Child's Book of Stories, 1914.
Illustrated by Jessie Willcox Smith

with her or to be turned into one of those unearthly monsters, like those he would have to pass by going into the castle.

"Ha! ha! ha! you make me laugh so that I can scarcely buckle the saddle-straps. I think I shall make it all right, my uncle, if I see a young lady there, you may depend."

"Well, my boy, I shall see how you will get on."

So he mounts his Arab steed, and off he goes like a shot out of a gun. At last he comes in sight of the castle. He ties his horse safe to a tree, and pulls out his watch. It was then a quarter to one, when he called out, "Swan, swan, carry me over, for the name of the old Griffin of the Greenwood." No sooner said than done. A swan under each side, and one in front, took him over in a crack. He got on his legs, and walked quietly by all those giants, lions, fiery serpents, and all manner of other frightful things too numerous to mention, while they were fast asleep, and that only for the space of one hour, when into the castle he goes neck or nothing. Turning to the right, upstairs he runs, and enters into a very grand bedroom, and sees a beautiful Princess lying full stretch on a gold bedstead, fast asleep. He gazed on her beautiful form with admiration, and he takes her garter off, and buckles it on his own leg, and he buckles his on hers; he also takes her gold watch and pocket-handkerchief, and exchanges his for hers; after that he ventures to give her a kiss, when she very nearly opened her eyes. Seeing the time short, off he runs downstairs, and passing through the kitchen to go into the garden for the apples, he could see the cook all-fours on her back on the middle of the floor, with the knife in one hand and the fork in the other. He found the apples, and filled the wallet; and on passing through the kitchen the cook near wakened, but he was obliged to make all the speed he possibly could, as the time was nearly up. He called out for the swans, and they managed to take him over; but they found that he was a little heavier than before. No sooner than he had mounted his horse he could hear a tremendous

He stood still in wonder and delight.
Nursery Tales, 1923.
Illustrated by Paul Woodroffe

He saw, upon a bed, the finest sight was ever beheld.

The Fairy Tales of Charles Perrault, 1922.

Illustrated by Harry Clarke

noise, the enchantment was broke, and they tried to follow him, but all to no purpose. He was not long before he came to the oldest brother's house; and glad enough he was to see it, for the sight and the noise of all those things that were after him nearly frightened him to death.

"Welcome, my boy; I am proud to see you. Dismount and put the horse in the stable, and come in and have some refreshments; I know you are hungry after all you have gone through in that castle. And tell me all you did, and all you saw there. Other kings' sons went by here to go to that castle, but they never came back alive, and you are the only one that ever broke the spell. And now you must come with me, with a sword in your hand, and must cut my head off, and must throw it in that well."

The young Prince dismounts, and puts his horse in the stable, and they go in to have some refreshments, for I can assure you he wanted some; and after telling everything that passed, which the old gentleman was very pleased to hear, they both went for a walk together, the young Prince looking around and seeing the place looking dreadful, as did the old man. He could scarcely walk from his toe-nails curling up like ram's horns that had not been cut for many hundred years, and big long hair. They come to a well, and the old man gives the Prince a sword, and tells him to cut his head off, and throw it in that well. The young man has to do it against his wish, but has to do it.

No sooner has he flung the head in the well, than up springs one of the finest young gentlemen you would wish to see; and instead of the old house and the frightful-looking place, it was changed into a beautiful hall and grounds. And they went back and enjoyed themselves well, and had a good laugh about the castle.

The young Prince leaves this young gentleman in all his glory, and he tells the young Prince before leaving that he will see him again before long. They have a jolly shake-hands, and off he goes to the next oldest brother; and, to make my long story short, he has to serve the other two brothers the same as the first.

Now the youngest brother began to ask him how things went on. "Did you see my two brothers?"

"Yes."

"How did they look?"

"Oh! they looked very well. I liked them much. They told me many things what to do."

"Well, did you go to the castle?"

"Yes, my uncle."

"And will you tell me what you see in there? Did you see the young lady?"

"Yes, I saw her, and plenty of other frightful things."

"Did you hear any snake biting you in my oldest brother's bed?"

"No, there were none there; I slept well."

"You won't have to sleep in the same bed to-night. You will have to cut my head off in the morning."

The young Prince had a good night's rest, and changed all the appearance of the place by cutting his friend's head off before he started in the morning.

No words cal tell how beautiful she was.
The Sleeping Beauty, 1920.
Illustrated by Arthur Rackham

And o'er his head, and round the bed, by the protecting Fairy led.
An Old Fairy Tale, 1868.
Illustrated by The Dalziel Brothers

A jolly shake-hands, and the uncle tells him it's very probable he shall see him again soon when he is not aware of it. This one's mansion was very pretty, and the country around it beautiful, after his head was cut off. Off Jack goes, over hills, dales, valleys, and mountains, and very near losing his apples again.

At last he arrives at the cross-roads, where he has to meet his brothers on the very day appointed. Coming up to the place, he sees no tracks of horses, and, being very tired, he lays himself down to sleep, by tying the horse to his leg, and putting the apples under his head. Presently up come the other brothers the same time to the minute, and found him fast asleep; and they would not waken him, but said one to another, "Let us see what sort of apples he has got under his head." So they took and tasted them, and found they were different to theirs. They took and changed his apples for theirs, and off to London as fast as they could, and left the poor fellow sleeping.

After a while he awoke, and, seeing the tracks of other horses, he mounted and off with him, not thinking anything about the apples being changed. He had still a long way to go, and by the time he got near London he could hear all the bells in the town ringing, but did not know what was the matter till he rode up to the palace, when he came to know that his father was recovered by his brothers' apples. When he got there his two brothers were off to some sports for a while; and the King was glad to see his youngest son, and very anxious to taste his apples. But when he found out that they were not good, and thought that they were more for poisoning him, he sent immediately for the headsman to behead his youngest son, who was taken away there and then in a carriage. But instead of the headsman taking his head off, he took him to a forest not far from the town, because he had pity on him, and there left him to take his chance, when presently up comes a big hairy bear, limping upon three legs. The Prince, poor fellow, climbed up a tree, frightened of him, but the bear told him to come down, that it was no use of him to stop there. With hard persuasion poor Jack comes down, and the bear speaks to him and bids him "Come here to me; I will not do you any harm. It's better for you to come with me and have some refreshments; I know that you are hungry all this time."

The poor young Prince says, "No, I am not hungry; but I was very frightened when I saw you coming to me first, as I had no place to run away from you."

The bear said, "I was also afraid of you when I saw that gentleman setting you down from the carriage. I thought you would have guns with you, and that you would not mind killing me if you saw me; but when I saw the gentleman going away with the carriage, and leaving you behind by yourself, I made bold to come to you, to see who you were, and now I know who you are very well. Are you not the king's youngest son? I have seen you and your brothers and lots of other gentlemen in this wood many times. Now before we go from here, I must tell you that I am in disguise; and I shall take you where we are stopping."

The young Prince tells him everything from first to last, how he started in search of the apples, and about the three old men, and about the castle, and how he was served at last by his father after he came home; and instead of the headsman taking his head off, he was kind enough to leave him his life, "and here I am now, under your protection."

The bear tells him, "Come on, my brother; there shall no harm come to you as long as you are with me."

So he takes him up to the tents; and when they see 'em coming, the girls begin to laugh, and say, "Here is our Jubal coming with a young gentleman." When he advanced nearer the tents, they all knew that he was the young Prince that had passed by that way many times before; and when Jubal went to change himself, he called most of them together into one tent, and told them all about him, and to be kind to him. And so they were, for there was nothing that he desired but what he had, the same as if he was in the palace with his father and

It's you my Prince.
Tales of Passed Times, 1900.
Illustrated by John Austin

mother. Jubal, after he pulled off his hairy coat, was one of the finest young men amongst them, and he was the young Prince's closest companion. The young Prince was always very sociable and merry, only when he thought of the gold watch he had from the young Princess in the castle, and which he had lost he knew not where.

He passed off many happy days in the forest; but one day he and poor Jubal were strolling through the trees, when they came to the very spot where they first met, and, accidentally looking up, he could see his watch hanging in the tree which he had to climb when he first saw poor Jubal coming to him in the form of a bear; and he cries out, "Jubal, Jubal, I can see my watch up in that tree."

"Well, I am sure, how lucky!" exclaimed poor Jubal; "shall I go and get it down?"

"No, I'd rather go myself," said the young Prince.

Now whilst all this was going on, the young Princess in that castle, seeing that one of the King of England's sons had been there by the changing of the watch and other things, got herself ready with a large army, and sailed off for England. She left her army a little out of the town, and she went with her guards straight up to the palace to see the King, and also demanded to see his sons. They had a long conversation together about different things. At last she demands one of the sons to come before her; and the oldest comes, when she asks him, "Have you ever been at the Castle of Melvales?" and he answers, "Yes." She throws down a pocket handkerchief and bids him to walk over it without stumbling. He goes to walk over it, and no sooner did he put his foot on it, than he fell down and broke his leg. He was taken off immediately and made a prisoner of by her own guards. The other was called upon, and was asked the same questions, and I had to go through the same performance, and

"It's you, O Prince, the youth of my dream!"
The Rainbow Book - Tales of Fun & Fancy, 1909.
Illustrated by Bernard Partridge

he also was made a prisoner of. Now she says, "Have you not another son?" when the King began so to shiver and shake and knock his two knees together that he could scarcely stand upon his legs, and did not know what to say to her, he was so much frightened. At last a thought came to him to send for his headsman, and inquire of him particularly, Did he behead his son, or was he alive?

"He is saved, O King."

"Then bring him here immediately, or else I shall be done for."

Two of the fastest horses they had were put in the carriage, to go and look for the poor Prince; and when they got to the very spot where they left him, it was the time when the Prince was up the tree, getting his watch down, and poor Jubal standing a distance off. They cried out to him, Had he seen another young man in this wood? Jubal, seeing such a nice carriage, thought something, and did not like to say No, and said Yes, and pointed up the tree; and they told him to come down immediately, as there was a young lady in search of him.

"Ha! ha! ha! Jubal, did you ever hear such a thing in all your life, my brother?"

"Do you call him your brother?"

"Well, he has been better to me than my brothers."

"Well, for his kindness he shall accompany you to the palace, and see how things turn out."

After they go to the palace, the Prince has a good wash, and appears before the Princess, when she asks him, Had he ever been at the Castle of Melvales?

Beauty-Awakened.
The Blue Fairy Book, 1922.
Illustrated by H. J. Ford

And in every room in the castle the people who had been lying asleep for a hundred years woke up.
The Sleeping Beauty, 1920.
Illustrated by Arthur Rackham

With a smile upon his face, he gives a graceful bow. And says my Lady, "Walk over that handkerchief without stumbling." He walks over it many times, and dances upon it, and nothing happened to him. She said, with a proud and smiling air, "That is the young man;" and out come the objects exchanged by both of them. Presently she orders a very large box to be brought in and to be opened, and out come some of the most costly uniforms that were ever worn on an emperor's back; and when he dressed himself up, the King could scarcely look upon him from the dazzling of the gold and diamonds on his coat. He orders his two brothers to be in confinement for a period of time; and before the Princess asks him to go with her to her own country, she pays a visit to the bear's camp, and she makes some very handsome presents for their kindness to the young Prince. And she gives Jubal an invitation to go with them, which he accepts; wishes them a hearty farewell for a while, promising to see them all again in some little time.

They go back to the King and bid farewell, and tell him not to be so hasty another time to order people to be beheaded before having a proper cause for it. Off they go with all their army with them; but while the soldiers were striking their tents, the Prince bethought himself of his Welsh harp, and had it sent for immediately to take with him in a beautiful wooden case. They called to see each of those three brothers whom the Prince had to stay with when he was on his way to the Castle of Melvales; and I can assure you, when they all got together, they had a very merry time of it. And there we will leave them.

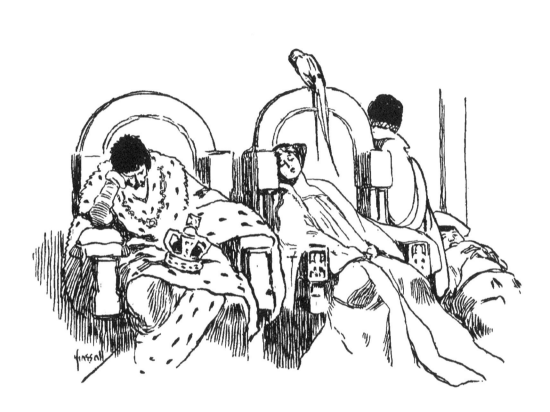

The Golden Age of Illustration

The 'Golden age of Illustration' refers to a period customarily defined as lasting from the latter quarter of the nineteenth century until just after the First World War. In this period of no more than fifty years the popularity, abundance and most importantly the unprecedented upsurge in quality of illustrated works marked an astounding change in the way that publishers, artists and the general public came to view this hitherto insufficiently esteemed art form.

Until the latter part of the nineteenth century, the work of illustrators was largely proffered anonymously, and in England it was only after Thomas Bewick's pioneering technical advances in wood engraving that it became common to acknowledge the artistic and technical expertise of book and magazine illustrators. Although widely regarded as the patriarch of the *Golden Age*, Walter Crane (1845-1915) started his career as an anonymous illustrator – gradually building his reputation through striking designs, famous for their sharp outlines and flat tints of colour. Like many other great illustrators to follow, Crane operated within many different mediums; a lifelong disciple of William Morris and a member of the Arts and Crafts Movement, he designed all manner of objects including wallpaper, furniture, ceramic ware and even whole interiors. This incredibly important and inclusive phase of British design proved to have a lasting impact on illustration both in the United Kingdom and Europe as well as America.

The artists involved in the Arts and Crafts Movement attempted to counter the ever intruding Industrial Revolution (the first wave of which lasted roughly from 1750-1850) by bringing the values of beautiful and inventive craftsmanship back into the sphere of everyday life. It must be noted that around the turn of the century the boundaries between what would today be termed 'fine art' as opposed to 'crafts' and 'design' were far more fluid and in many cases non-operational, and many illustrators had lucrative painterly careers in addition to their design work. The Romanticism of the *Pre Raphaelite Brotherhood* combined with the intricate curvatures of the *Art Nouveaux* movement provided influential strands running through most illustrators work. The latter especially so for the Scottish illustrator Anne Anderson (1874-1930) as well as the Dutch artist Kay Nielson (1886-1957), who was also inspired by the stunning work of Japanese artists such as Hiroshige.

One of the main accomplishments of nineteenth century illustration lay in its ability to reach far wider numbers than the traditional 'high arts'. In 1892 the American critic William A. Coffin praised the new medium for popularising art; 'more has been done through the medium of illustrated literature... to make the masses of people realise that there is such a thing as art and that it is worth caring about'. Commercially, illustrated publications reached their zenith with the burgeoning 'Gift Book' industry which emerged in the first decade of the twentieth century. The first widely distributed gift book was published in 1905. It comprised of Washington Irving's short story *Rip Van Winkle* with the addition of 51 colour plates by a true master of illustration; Arthur Rackham. Rackham created each plate by first painstakingly drawing his subject in a sinuous pencil line before applying an ink layer – then he used layer upon layer of delicate watercolours to build up the romantic yet calmly ethereal results on which his reputation was constructed. Although Rackham is now one of the most recognisable names in illustration, his delicate palette owed no small debt to Kate Greenaway (1846-1901) – one of the first female illustrators whose pioneering and incredibly subtle use of the watercolour medium resulted in her election to the Royal Institute of Painters in Water Colours in 1889.

The year before Arthur Rackam's illustrations for *Rip Van Winkle* were published, a young and aspiring French artist by the name of Edmund Dulac (1882-1953) came to London and was to create a similarly impressive legacy. His timing could not have been more fortuitous. Several factors converged around the turn of the century which allowed illustrators and publishers alike a far greater freedom of creativity than previously imagined. The origination of the 'colour separation' practice meant that colour images, extremely faithful to the original artwork could be produced on a grand scale. Dulac possessed a rigorously painterly background (more so than his contemporaries) and was hence able to utilise the new technology so as to allow the colour itself to refine and define an object as opposed to the traditional pen and ink line. It has been estimated that in 1876 there was only one 'colour separation' firm in London, but by 1900 this number had rocketed to fifty. This improvement in printing quality also meant a reduction in labour, and coupled with the introduction of new presses and low-cost supplies of paper this meant that publishers could for the first time afford to pay high wages for highly talented artists.

Whilst still in the U.K, no survey of the *Golden Age of Illustration* would be complete without a mention of the Heath-Robinson brothers. Charles Robinson was renowned for his beautifully detached style, whether in pen and ink or sumptuous watercolours. Whilst William (the youngest) was to later garner immense fame for his carefully constructed yet tortuous machines operated by comical, intensely serious attendants. After World War One the Robinson brothers numbered among the few artists of the Golden Age who continued to regularly produce illustrated works. As we move towards the United States, one illustrator - Howard Pyle (1853-1911) stood head and shoulders above his contemporaries as the most distinguished illustrator of the age. From 1880 onwards Pyle illustrated over 100 volumes, yet it was not quantity which ensured his precedence over other American (and European) illustrators, but quality.

Pyle's sumptuous illustrations benefitted from a meticulous composition process livened with rich colour and deep recesses, providing a visual framework in which tales such as *Robin Hood* and *The Four Volumes of the Arthurian Cycle* could come to life. These are publications which remain continuous good sellers up till the present day. His flair and originality combined with a thoroughness of planning and execution were principles which he passed onto his many pupils at the *Drexel Institute of Arts and Sciences*. Two such pupils were Jessie Willcox Smith (1863-1935) who went on to illustrate books such as *The Water Babies* and *At the Back of North Wind* and perhaps most famously Maxfield Parrish (1870-1966) who became famed for luxurious colour (most remarkably demonstrated in his blue paintings) and imaginative designs; practices in no short measure gleaned from his tutor. As an indication of Parrish's popularity, in 1925 it was estimated that one fifth of American households possessed a Parrish reproduction.

As is evident from this brief introduction to the 'Golden Age of Illustration', it was a period of massive technological change and artistic ingenuity. The legacy of this enormously important epoch lives on in the present day – in the continuing popularity and respect afforded to illustrators, graphic and fine artists alike. This *Origins of Fairy Tales from Around the World* series will hopefully provide a fascinating insight into an era of intense historical and creative development, bringing both little known stories, and the art that has accompanied them, back to life.

CPSIA information can be obtained
at www.ICGtesting.com
Printed in the USA
BVHW021605010619
549794BV00026B/139/P